The Forgiveness GAME

NORMA MCLAUCHLIN

Chosen Pen Publishing
Fayetteville, NC

ISBN: 978-1-952315-48-0
LCCP: 2022916020

The Forgiveness Game/ Norma McLauchlin
1. Literary Collections–Fiction–African
American
2. Fiction-Spiritual and Religion
3. Fiction-Christian Suspense
4. Fiction – Christian Romance

To order additional copies of the resource, write Chosen Pen Customer Service:
1420 Hoke Loop Road
Fayetteville, NC 28314
FAX orders to 910-868-3300
Phone orders to 910-818-6652

Website: www.chosepen.com
www.chosenpenacademy.com

Printed in the United States of America

DEDICATION

To my husband, Pastor Allen S. McLauchlin, Th.D., who has supported my work in countless ways, especially as I walk in my God-given gifts.

To my son Scotty and grandchildren Haven, Eden, and Khari McLauchlin, for loving me for who I am. Thank you for believing in me and for being the individuals that you are.

To my family, my mom - the late Early Miller Tucker, my Father the late Oscar Otis Tucker, my sisters the late Brenda Tucker Purcell and Karen Angela Tucker, my niece Radiah Cerice Spleen, my nephew Oscar Gregory Purcell, my grand niece and nephew Cierra Marie Spleen and Christopher Spleen, Goddaughters Alison Bryant Thor, Christel Bryant, Helisha Dawn McLauchlin, April Elina McLauchlin, Jocelyn Gladney, David Bernard Gladney, and Diantha Gladney Jones, my spiritual daughters, Trazzia Wallace and LaSherra Lee, and my Literary Mentor, Joylynn M. Ross, your presence in my life has made it what it is today.

Above all, I thank God for allowing me to write this book.

CHAPTER ONE

It was another rainy day in Decatur, Georgia. I left the hospital in a dizzy froth of madness and flew home on two wheels and a prayer. Pulling my car into the driveway with a screeching halt, I jumped out, slammed the door closed, then ran across the rain-soaked front yard into the house. I was in too much of a hurry to park in the garage. I was on a mission.

Slipping and sliding down the hallway in soggy heels, I tore through my bedroom and dashed to the nightstand beside my bed. I used it to brace my fall while reaching to retrieve the Sampson family Bible I always kept there. I opened it to reveal the hiding place for my purple Beretta and a box of 45-caliber bullets. With shaky hands, I loaded the gun. I also grabbed my New International Version Study Bible . . . so I could read scripture over my son-in-law Bounce's, dead body when I finished with him.

Not speaking to anyone, I sprinted back through the puddles of water I had left in the hallway. After righting myself from a near tumble, I rushed back out into the storm.

The torrential Georgian storm hailed against me as I worked to open the door of the driver's side of the car. In one hand, I gripped the loaded gun; in the other, I tried to lift the door handle.

But the door handle was slippery, and the mighty gusts of wind threatened to knock over my petite, 145- pound frame. My long, mid-back-length hair whipped around my face, blocking my view of the handle while I struggled to get inside. I staggered back when the door flew backward; pushing against the wind, I inched forward.

My tan and black maxi dress was soaking wet and clung to my pecan-tan skin. While my tan platform heels sank into the rich earth, I rocked my curvy hips back and forth to slide under the steering wheel that I had set too low, but my last step had my left heel still stuck in the mud, and it wasn't giving. I viciously kicked out as hard as I could. My shoe landed in the grass near the front door, and I fell backward onto the seat and exhaled as I finally slid all of me into place.

I was now with one shoe on, the other off. Shaking the right shoe free, I was now barefoot, and while I usually drive in flats with a pillow behind my back, this wasn't working well because I forgot my key ingredient. In my panic, I forgot the pillow, and it helped me move closer to the pedals.

Yes, this is called "short-person blues," and it's real. But I'm so distraught today that none of the "usuals" are happening. I'm figuring things out as I go. Finally, under the steering wheel of my new 1976 black Cadillac Seville, I take a moment to exhale.

At five feet even, my hair hangs past my shoulders, hitting me midback. No weave either—like most Black folks, I claim Indigenous ancestry—don't judge. But these apple bottom hips? They're my daddy's mama's and her down-home Alabama roots. Since I was a teen, I've been dragging this wagon behind me, and it only gets more prominent with age.

And like my ancestors before me, I'm on a hunt. The

varmint I'm hunting is Bounce, my son-in-law. I'd gotten word that he had beaten my daughter, Patsy, the older of my two children, and put her in the hospital. She was a patient at Emory Decatur Hospital due to Bounce's physical abuse.

I planned to find and then kill him. Vengeance is mine, so saith the Lord and a person's mother. (I know the scripture doesn't exactly say that, but *she's* my baby.) I think both are equally righteous.

"Bang!"

Startled, I jumped at the loud slap on my window. Looming over the car was my husband of twenty-five years, Malcolm. His face was thunderous. And the way he was panting, he must have sprinted from the house. Knowing he now had my attention; he jumped in the car's passenger side and slammed the door shut.

"Get out of this car right now, Trish. I know you have the Bible with the hidden gun in it," he shouted. "I saw you racing out of the house. And knowing you, I checked, and it's gone. So, give it to me right now. You're not shooting anyone!"

I rolled my hazel eyes at Malcolm for dripping water onto my new leather seat and daring to tell me what to do.

I know I was dripping first, but it's my car.

"Stop trying to control me," I growled, working to hold back the nausea that continued to creep up my throat.

Picturing this monster's hands around my child's neck . . . made me want to vomit.

"He put his hands on my baby, bruised, and abused her, and you want me to stand by and let that happen? Why are *you* letting this happen? I'm going to make sure he has breakfast with the devil—" My tirade was interrupted by my own loud wailing. Breathless with anger and bulging, bloodshot eyes, my stomach churned, threatening to spew my entire breakfast. My heart was beating irregularly, and I had to slow it down for fear I was having a heart attack. I clutched my chest, breathing deeply and muttering incoherently, "Don't you understand? Bounce beat my child, my daughter—*our* daughter."

The lavender and eucalyptus mixed air freshener hanging on the rearview mirror tried to help me find a place of calmness.

I snorted, thinking, *"All the lavender- scent hype is a lie."*

Because after two or three moments of inhaling and attempting to calm myself, I screamed, "My only daughter, Malcolm. I can't bear it."

Malcolm opened his mouth to speak, but I wasn't done. I couldn't understand why he wasn't riding shotgun with me. Shouldn't he understand?

"No, Malcolm, I'm not finished. My only son is in the military and deployed out of the country. I constantly fear that he will be shipped home in a box or not return home the same. This added pressure from Bounce and Patsy may mentally push me over the edge," I said with pleading eyes.

"You *do* know these are *my* kids too? I'm trying to understand you, Trish. First off, I live with that same fear for MJ. Don't forget *I* served in the army and have firsthand knowledge of the life of a soldier. But I'm choosing to trust God and pray that MJ returns unharmed and without post-traumatic stress disorder (PTSD). But if he does, God will give us the strength to handle it. Second, it's not your job or assignment to shoot Bounce."

I was appalled, and I had listened to Malcolm, but visions of the six-foot-six, two- hundred-pound man's muscular body straddling my daughter's tiny, four-foot- nine-inch body while slamming his meaty fists into her body looped in through my frazzled mind like a reel. Bounce had to pay. *He deserves to die, God!*

"I'm not going to shoot him. I'm going to kill him. And don't try to stop me, Malcolm!"

I searched my husband's face with desperate eyes. Exasperated, I growled.

"How can you be so quiet about this? What's *wrong* with you?"

Malcolm sighed as though the world had settled heavily on his ample shoulders. He bowed his head... I waited. I assumed he was asking God for strength. Then he spoke softly but firmly.

"Give me the gun. If anyone kills him, it will be me. There was a time when I would have already taken him out. You know where I'm from and how hard I fought to change my reactive mentality. With my military training, it would only take a little push to send me over the edge. I'm her father. God assigned her to me for protection. He assigned her to you for instruction. Now, in this season where I profess to follow Christ, you want me to abandon that which was so hard won?" Malcolm tried to take my hand, but I held it away.

"Baby, He also taught me to let Him handle my problems. It's hard, but I'm trying to honor God and do what He expects from me as head of my household."

I looked out the window, watched the droplets hit the pane, and wondered if my throbbing headache pounded in sync with each drip. It seemed as though it did. Malcolm pulled me back into our conversation with his next comments.

"You know I have the call and desire to preach the gospel," Malcolm said. "You are involved in leading women through Bible study," he continued. "We'd never forgive ourselves if we turn our backs on God when tough times came. We must be an example for others to follow. Trish, give me the gun. Murder isn't you, sweetheart! Living a godly life is what we've promised to do."

My incoherent sobs and muffled exclamations filled the car.

In a tender voice, Malcolm pleaded, "I plan to grow old with you, woman, and we can't do that in jail. Let's get the police involved. We cannot handle this ourselves."

"Police? Bounce is a Black man. The worst the police will do is give him a beat down."

When Malcolm looked at me in disbelief at my statement, I reluctantly amended it.

"Okay, maybe they would kill him if it wasn't a Black woman he had beaten. But my Patsy is a Black woman. So, since your beliefs won't let you handle this, I need to handle this myself." I looked at the man of my heart and willed him to let me go.

I could feel my heart hardening. My bulging eyes and scowling face showed my lack of desire to reason with him any longer. Instead, I wanted gangster action from the pre-saved Malcolm against the fool who had broken my daughter's body.

"For whatever reason, this is not you taking action, but me, Malcolm." I screeched. "I'm an angry Black mother. He hurt my child," I sniffled. "He hurt my baby."

Malcolm shook his head at me as though he couldn't understand my reasoning, while I did not understand his. We were at an impasse. I would try one more time.

"Patsy's face was unrecognizable, Malcolm. Her swollen-shut eyes were purple and black to match the rest of her body. A stiff white cast encased her right arm and left leg. Without her name on the door, I wouldn't have known it was my Patsy."

Feeling my tears tracing through what makeup foundation the rain hadn't washed from my face, I struggled to catch my breath. Why did this happen to my Patsy?

"I was there, Trish. I might not have stayed long. But I saw. It's why I had to leave, go to the church, and lie on the altar. I couldn't let the anger I see consuming you consume me. Trish, please. Can't we just talk about this?" Malcolm's eyes were loaded with tears.

"I've done enough talking," I wiped my face. "It's time for action."

Clutching the gun in my trembling hand, I struggled to put the key into the ignition with the other hand.

"Malcolm, he's going to die today. Stop trying to stop me. I should be holding you back, not you telling me to calm down. What's wrong with you?"

"Woman, did you *not* hear anything I said? Has your anger made you deaf? She's *my* daughter too," Malcolm proclaimed. "You have to know that my love for God allows me to see my angels battling the legions of demons on my behalf. Satan doesn't want us to win this fight. If we kill Bounce, we are no better than he is. Our testimony will be of no effect. We will not be able to help bring anyone into the Kingdom. Please, open your heart, Trish, to recognize this is spiritual warfare."

"I don't care about spiritual warfare. Where were Patsy's angels when Bounce beat her? Absent. They didn't show up. That's why this is my battle. I don't care about what others think. I only want revenge for the wrong done to my Patsy. Don't you remember the Bible also teaches an eye for an eye? That's what I'm trying to do. I'm going back to the Old Testament. A beat down for a beat down." My voice strained as I screamed against the crackling of the thunderous sound of the pounding rain.

Using one of his military-trained maneuvers, Malcolm

suddenly snatched the gun from my hand, released the magazine, checked, and cleared the weapon, then pulled me over the gearshift onto his large lap in what seemed like one motion.

Shocked and helpless, I screamed, "No," pounding my hands against his chest. "Give it back to meeeee . . ." I clawed at his arms, snot rolling down my face. I struggled, but my efforts were fruitless.

"Stop it, Trish." Malcolm gathered me in his viselike solid arms, rocking me as he crooned. "I got you. Let me handle it." Despite my screaming, Malcolm's voice was calm.

How could you? How could you?

Swallowing my despair, I closed my swollen, bloodshot eyes and swallowed my pain. Nothing will ever be the same again. My Patsy's mental problems would only intensify with such a traumatic experience. Why couldn't he see?

Sitting in rain-soaked clothes, I tried to explain. "Malcolm, please listen to me," I begged. "Adding this abuse to Patsy's current struggles will break her. She'll feel unloved and worthless. How do we know she won't get depressed or attempt suicide?"

"Trish, do you think killing her husband will pull her away from a breakdown or closer to it?" Malcolm asked.

I couldn't hear his reasoning, so I yelled while he ignored me. Finally, I fought him, slamming my head against his chest and kicking him with my bare feet. Malcolm wouldn't give me what I wanted despite my efforts to free myself. He wouldn't release me to drive my car, look for Bounce, and kill him. Still, I raised my voice until it was nearly gone.

Malcolm remained eerily silent during my attack. Somewhere in the back of my head, I knew how hard it was for him to console me while trying to understand how his son-in-law could hurt his daughter. But I felt like he felt . . . He could do nothing about it except keep me from committing a crime and spending the rest of my life in prison.

He tightened his grip on me, stroking my hair with a deep sigh. "I love you, Trish. Please believe me when I tell you that God promises there will be sunshine on the other side of this situation."

That's not what I wanted to hear. I caught a second wind and started grappling with Malcolm again, but I was no match for my strong husband. He overpowered me and took control of my body. Finally, I collapsed against him in defeat. Sitting there limp and weak, I slumped against Malcolm's soft, brown, and red wet mohair sweater.

"You can't see it now, baby, but God will handle this. It's not too hard for Him," Malcolm said as he tightened his embrace.

"As your husband, I'm your protector. So please don't make me barricade you in our bedroom tonight. Please understand that no matter what, I will love you the same as Christ loves the church. I'll lay down my life for you, Trish. So, I'll do whatever it takes to keep you safe, whether it be from someone else or yourself."

While I appreciated Malcolm's love for me and the Lord, I wanted nothing to do with God or His word. I certainly didn't want anything to do with his legion of angels. I swear I felt the Holy Spirit tapping me on the shoulder to break through my madness. Vengeance belongs to God (as the Spirit reminded me), but the thief who came to steal, kill, and destroy had a grip on me. I was bent on anger and revenge. So, amid Malcolm and my conscience trying to reason with me, I was busy developing a plan for Bounce's demise. Therefore, unfortunately, I forgot to leave it up to God.

Yes, today, Satan . . .

CHAPTER TWO

An hour earlier, Malcolm and I sat in our kitchen and enjoyed one of my home-cooked dinners. I prepared my specialty: fried chicken and gravy, macaroni, and cheese, (I carried the title "Best-Tasting Mac and Cheese" at our church), fried cabbage, rice, Southern corn bread, and sweet tea. A homemade hot apple pie was for dessert.

"Yes, sweetheart," to quote my grandmother, "ooh wee, babyy, you put your foot in that meal. Everything was delicious." Rubbing his stomach, Malcolm said,

"You certainly know how to keep your man happy," as he stood and smooched my cheek.

While eating, I realized I felt pleased with our life as empty nesters. With both children no longer living at home, I felt contentment and peace in my current relationship with my husband. Standing to clear the table, I hugged his broad shoulders and gave him a pat on the rear as he left the kitchen to attend the men's meeting at our church.

After preparing hot, sudsy water in the kitchen sink, I began to wash our dinner dishes, thinking how little there was to clean for two people. Looking out of the kitchen window, past the yellow curtains that had been there since we moved in, I wondered at the rain. I enjoyed watching the rain's constant beat against the windowpane. Along with the lavender-scented candles burning throughout the house, the rain was soothing to my spirit.

During my Google research for ways to help keep Patsy calm, I read several articles. I loved to meditate and spend time with God during thunderstorms. I thanked Him for the awesomeness of how He created the world and provided all within it. Finally, I said a silent prayer of thanks for the part I played in His sovereign plan.

While washing the dinner dishes, I admired the daisies sitting so prettily in their crystal vase on the windowsill. Daisies were my favorite flower, and Malcolm had given me the flowers earlier that day. He gave them to me, "Just because I love our life together," he said. That made me go into the kitchen and start pulling food together to provide my husband with a wonderful dinner for his thoughtfulness.

Since my life was so peaceful and filled with my husband's love, I began to plan the next midweek Bible study with the women who enjoyed digging deeper into the word like me. I enjoyed teaching it. I planned to teach a lesson about what happens to Christ's followers for eternity. Bible open, my phone rang. When I picked it up to answer, everything in my world shifted.

"Hello?"

"Hey, Trish. Ummm, are you busy?" "Hey, Carolyn, no. I'm going to do some Bible studying, but I always have time for you."

"I don't know how to tell you this, girl, but Patsy is in the hospital."

Carolyn was Patsy's godmother and my best friend. It wasn't unusual for Patsy to end up in the hospital, because for the last ten years she had experienced mental health issues and manic episodes. Sometimes because Carolyn was so close to Patsy, she knew things before I did. So, while I was bracing myself for more mental health counseling visits to attempt to help Patsy, I wasn't alarmed . . . until the phone became silent. Now, this phone call felt different, and my apprehension rose.

"Carolyn?"

"Trish, listen to me," Carolyn said hurriedly. "It's more than that this time. Bounce beat Patsy, and it's bad." She pronounced each word slowly. Carolyn's trembling voice said she wasn't exaggerating.

"What do you mean, Bounce beat her?" I stammered. "He wouldn't ever put his hands on Patsy. There's no way Bounce would hurt my daughter. He's the perfect husband," I shrieked in disbelief.

"The perfect husband?" Carolyn blasted. The tension in her voice cut through the line.

"You mean to tell me Patsy has never told you about their fights? This isn't the first-time things have gotten physical between them, girl." Carolyn paused and took a deep breath. "The two of them have been in more fights than I can count, but it's never been as bad as this."

I knew Bounce had been nothing shy of amazing to Patsy. He'd always been respectful to her and made it seem like there wasn't anything he wouldn't do for my daughter. He was constantly showering Patsy with love, gifts, and respect. I loved Bounce like a son . . . at least until now. The more Carolyn explained, the more perplexed I became. "Are you sure about this, Carolyn?" It sounded like she was speaking in a foreign language. "How do you know this?"

Carolyn hesitated, then said, "Patsy's told me about their fights more than once. I thought you knew."

"Why didn't you tell me?" I directed the question more at myself than at Carolyn. "And why didn't she come to me herself?" I howled. "*You're* not her mother. What kind of friend are you? I expect more from her godmother. Tell me right now what you did to help my Patsy."

"Why are you asking me about this, Trish?" She was so casual about it and talked so much around me. "Patsy didn't ask me not to share it. So, I assumed she discussed it with you too," Carolyn sighed. She then shared, "I promise I didn't realize you weren't aware of all this. I thought you never brought it up because it embarrassed you that Patsy stayed with Bounce. I know how you feel about physical abuse against women."

"I have to get to my grandbabies," I thought out loud.

"I have them; don't worry," Carolyn said.

"Sweet Jesus, did they see what happened? I'll be right there."

Carolyn yelled. "Trish? Trish! The kids are okay. Patsy asked me to pick them up from school, and when I pulled up and saw the door was wide open, I knew something was wrong. I had them stay in the car when I went inside and found her."

"But then they saw their mother taken away in an ambulance? Carolyn, they must be traumatized."

"No, they didn't see. I had them go into Ms. Mable's house next door. She looked like she knew something had happened but was scared to check it out. She took them in her kitchen for a snack."

"She *thought* but didn't check?"

Carolyn exhaled loudly. "Trish, come on now. Ms. Mable is seventy-five years old. She lives alone, and what she must hear from there on the regular has taught her to mind her own business. As a matter of fact, one day, I heard Patsy tell her to do just that."

"I'll come and get the kids after I go and see Patsy," I relented.

"Wouldn't it be better to leave them with me for a few days while you guys get things settled? I know you will spend a lot of time at the hospital."

Someone had to catch my building fury. "Well, I guess that's why Patsy picked to talk to you. You just have all the answers!"

As the realization set in, I held the phone away from my ear and smashed it against the kitchen's marble countertop, watching it break into tiny pieces. Bounce had hurt my daughter.

Hold on, Patsy, Mama is on her way. Blinking, I sat back and peered at Malcolm, who had walked back into the room and stared back at me. I had thoughtlessly placed the phone on speaker to continue setting up the table for my study time. I snatched a clean dishtowel from the kitchen counter and dried the tears drenching his cheeks. I trembled at the news. In my pain, I failed to realize that although his flesh was suffering, he felt the hope of a Christ follower. Unlike me, Malcolm put his trust and faith in God and trusted He would work things out for our good.

I placed my arms around him, listening to his heartbeat and remembering when we were in love, and we cuddled as the rain pounded against the roof. We didn't know it, but we had no real problems back then, just how much to save and where to raise a family when we had one. While I wondered where we may have gone wrong as parents, Malcolm must have wondered how God would work it out for our good. But unfortunately, I couldn't see any good in what happened to Patsy coming to pass.

First, I reflected on my friend Carolyn's words. *It's happened numerous times.* Then like a movie, the footage was rewound of Bounce and Patsy's courtship, and I envisioned what had led to this moment in time as though I were in the front-row seat of their lives.

CHAPTER THREE

ounce Brown is sixteen years older than my daughter, Patsy. He and I grew up in the same neighborhood; we attended the same elementary school and church. Ours was a loving community where our neighbors, schoolteachers, and pastors helped raise us.

We had the village other folks just talked about. Whatever happened at school was relayed to our parents, aunts, uncles, and every adult in the neighborhood. Rest assured, the whooping was coming anywhere along the way home, where your parents gave the ultimate punishment. The worst was on Sunday when the preacher called you in front of the church to have one of the deacons pray over you to cast out the demon that caused whatever sin you committed tempt you again.

I moved from Decatur years ago, but I remember the first time I saw Bounce once we moved back home. He still looked the same, just older. Tall and dark as night, with a full beard and big brown eyes. All muscles, he was in great physical shape, with no body fat. I knew he came from a good, well- mannered family, and everyone spoke highly of him. Bounce was an above-average student who never got into trouble and made a success of himself. So, it surprised no one that he owned ten car dealerships in ten states because he always focused on his businesses. But of course, I hadn't counted on Bounce falling in love with my Patsy.

Folks around Decatur were in awe of Bounce and Patsy's relationship, but our friends and family were skeptical, given their enormous age gap. I couldn't blame Bounce for being smitten with my favorite girl, though. Pasty was beautiful, with her honey- tinted skin, head full of soft, jet-black curls, almond-shaped eyes, wide hips, and a round butt like mine. And her smile. I've always loved Patsy's smile, equivalent to a warm summer day. To catch even a snippet of it could warm anybody's heart.

That smile is what caught Bounce's attention. Despite their differences, I respected Patsy's decision to enter a relationship with him. She was grown enough to decide who she wanted to marry. I couldn't interfere with that. Honestly, I respected Bounce for tending to Patsy's needs and treating her like a princess. Who doesn't want their child loved the way he loved her?

But life can change in an instant. What did the commercial tout? *Life comes at you fast.* We went from line dancing at Bounce and Patsy's wedding reception to Pasty being hospitalized and diagnosed with mental health bipolar schizoaffective disorder. Issues. She was just a 22-year-old newlywed when she experienced her first episode.

How long has Bounce been beating Patsy? Is he the reason for her challenges?

I came from a family living with mental illness. As small children, my sister and two brothers knew my uncle June Bug was different. It was apparent every time he became agitated for no reason, cursing and striking out at us. We knew then to keep our distance from him because he would curse and try to hit us. My grandparents usually locked him in his room during these episodes.

Then there was my cousin Josie, who spent her adult life in a mental institution. My parents allowed me to accompany them once when they visited her. I remember wondering why she never spoke, just stared at us as if she did not recognize her family. My father later explained that the institution kept the patients heavily medicated for their safety and that of others.

Although I knew that science declared mental illness was not hereditary, I took the gamble that the same illnesses that affected my family members would affect my daughter, but I lost. In my eyes and heart, it's a familial curse passed down from generation to generation. Lord knows I tried and prayed, but nothing worked. Still, since her diagnosis, I'd been right by Patsy's side for the last ten years, through the extreme swings from high and low.

~~~~

The hurt of seeing the child who has already gone through so much lying in an ICU hospital bed tore me apart. Malcolm held my hand as we looked down at Patsy. She had always been a robust girl, curvy and full of life, but the sallowness of her skin and the tubes running in and out of her body were signs that she had taken a beating that could have taken her out.

"How is she really, Nurse?" I asked as the nurse stood in the doorway.

"She's sedated so that she can heal. It's a good thing. We don't expect her to wake up until tomorrow. Today is for her to rest and begin the process."

Malcolm nodded. "Thank you. As her parents, if there are any changes at all, we would like to be contacted."

The nurse gave a small smile. "We appreciate having close family members to support her. She'll need you in the coming days. She'll have a fight on her hands."
~~~~

The nurse then completed checking her vitals and left the room. Hearing a sob, I turned and watched as my mighty man of God fell to his knees by his baby girl's bed. I followed close behind him as he prayed aloud, and I tried—I really did—to follow the prayer. But all I could see was red. When I noted the bruising over her face that the bandages couldn't hide, I saw red. When I saw the casts holding together broken bones, my red haze turned to flames consuming my sight. As Malcolm prayed, I raged.

Malcolm stood, kissing her hands around the lines that were providing her with drugs to allow her to rest. "I'm going to Uber to the church. I need to get to the altar, and I'll call some deacons to meet me there. Stay as long as you need to, baby. I'll be back." He hugged me tight and then looked sorrowfully back at our baby as he left the room.

I nodded, not really hearing him. I sat there, rocking in my misery, wondering where I had gone wrong. How could this serpent be let into our family? How had I missed the signs of abusive behavior? And why didn't Patsy trust me enough to share her pain?

As I sat, I spoke to her about better times. I reminded her of the strength that she had shown, fighting for her peace for ten years, and I wouldn't let her give up. Instead, I would pray her free. I watched as she showed no sign of hearing me, but I talked until I couldn't anymore. I then sat and pondered how this could happen. But the longer I sat, the more I became agitated. I knew I had stewed too long when the nursing staff returned to check her vitals and administer more sedatives in the plastic pouch above her head.

I silently rose from my seat and moved toward the door. I didn't want to leave her behind, but I had business to attend to for all of us. I had decided to kill Bounce somewhere between a sob and a curse.

Storming out of the hospital, I thanked God Malcolm left me the car. I knew if I ran home, I could get my gun before he arrived. If I delayed, Malcolm might interfere. He wasn't the man I had once married. I had thought that was a good thing in the past, but in the present, I wanted the thug.

~~~~

The car windows were fogged as I remembered how our day started, right up to my butt going to sleep on Malcolm's lap. Sighing, I noticed the rain had finally subsided. I turned my head, staring into Malcolm's eyes. "All those times Patsy fell apart and ended up in the hospital, do you think it was because of Bounce?"

Malcolm's eyes mirrored mine, relaying the same thoughts. "I don't know, Pumpkin."

"Humph. All the time we kept the children when Patsy was in the hospital for weeks on end so Bounce could stay with her every time."

Malcolm nodded. "He even gave us more money than it took to care for the kids, even when we didn't need it."

A calculating glint twinkled from my eyes. "Guilt money, I know it. All from Bounce's guilty conscience, and we accepted it."

"We don't know that for sure, baby. Let's get more information before we follow this too far down this road," Malcolm said, still stroking my hair. Since it comforted him, I didn't complain that he was messing up my hair. I felt this because I could feel the tension in his body, and I knew Malcolm was restraining himself from hurting Bounce the way I wanted him to and that he was just keeping me calm. He thought one of us needed to stay out of jail.

I unlocked the door and slung it open. Then I slid off Malcolm's lap and hopped out of the car. The rain had subsided, but the thunder remained in my heart. Malcolm followed me toward the house as I headed to the back kitchen door. I looked back and saw his hand
~~~~

tremble as he secured the gun inside his jacket pocket. A frightening reel passed before my eyes, showing Malcolm morphing into a gangster, and killing Bounce.

"You don't have to worry, Malcolm. I will not fight you for the gun."

"Good. One of us needs to remain in our right mind."

I opened the door and slammed it shut, not stopping to pick up my shoes from the yard. In my bare feet, I stomped and tracked mud onto the kitchen floor. I found the nearest chair, plopped down in a huff, and began to shiver. That's when I realized my clothes were soaked and sticking to my body. Too tired to move, I sat there and reminisced about Patsy's married life. I thought about how I'd pray over my daughter, her husband, and my grandchildren for ten years. Yet, after what Bounce had done, although I wanted him to get what he deserved, the first thought that came out of my mouth shocked me.

I feel sorry for him.

"Bounce married a beautiful, vibrant, amazing woman. But unfortunately, he didn't sign up to deal with Patsy's multiple personalities," I murmured.

Malcolm grunted in satisfaction. "That's the woman I know. Let's take a moment to walk through all of it. Somewhere is the truth."

Admitting out loud that I sympathized with him, my daughter's attack tasted like acid shooting up my throat.

Unbelievable!

Seeming to read my mind, Malcolm said, "Guilt is a toxic worm weaving itself in and out of your system. Don't do it, Trisha. Let's sleep on this tonight and tackle it in the morning." Malcolm leaned against the counter with his arms folded. "Our minds should be clearer then."

I glanced at my tall, handsome, clean- shaven husband. He handled this well. I didn't even have enough energy to stand. I was emotionally and mentally depleted; I just wanted all this to be a lie. It took years for me to accept Patsy's illness. I blamed myself and my family for her condition. She'd been a happy child, a charismatic teenager, and a loving young adult who was nothing like the woman she had turned into. She'd become an abused woman without me knowing.

I hoisted myself from the chair and lumbered toward our bedroom.

"I'm going to run a hot bath and soak for eternity."

"I'll be there in a minute," Malcolm called out as he walked to the opposite end of the hallway that led to our guest rooms. Since he didn't put the gun back on the nightstand beside our bed, I knew he was looking for a place to hide it.

Finally stripping from my wet, smelly clothes, I said dejectedly, "Hide it well, Malcolm." Malcolm's boots hitting the hardwood floors was his response.

Before entering the bathroom, I prayed, "Please, God, give me a moment of peace." Then I waited for the urging of the Holy Spirit. Since my spirit remained quiet after three minutes, "I assume your answer is no," I said to myself. A single tear trickled down my cheek and onto my chest.

I lit lavender-scented candles to help calm me. I had read that the scent of lavender provided a sense of peace for those with mental illnesses, so I kept it in all the rooms of my house and encouraged Patsy to use what I left at her home as well.

Looking at myself in the mirror over the sink, I felt so alone and dejected that I beat my fist against its marble top. I felt no relief after not hearing from God. I was so distraught that I picked up the ceramic toothbrush holder and threw it at my reflection in the mirror, shattering it. The broken pieces were like my heart. I had failed Patsy. I couldn't keep her safe.

Stepping gingerly over the broken glass, I lowered myself into the tub. After sinking into the Jacuzzi tub filled with warm, lavender-scented water and bubbles, I could no longer hold in my rage toward God.

"Why, Lord, why didn't you keep my daughter safe? You promised you would supply all my needs. And now, all I need is for Patsy to be safe," I shouted. "You are not a promise keeper. Why are you hiding Bounce from me? He's nothing—an enormous pile of nothing. A woman beater, and he better stay away from my daughter. When will you become *my* Jehovah-Jireh?"

Of course, I failed to consider my part in the promise. God's promises always have a condition.

As I continued with my bath, I became more enraged toward God and Bounce. However, for a quick second, I couldn't help but be upset with Patsy for allowing Bounce to abuse her physically and continue a relationship with him. However, it passed as quickly as it came. It washed down the drain with the water as I stepped from the tub.

CHAPTER FOUR

fter my bath, I slipped into my bathrobe and sat on the side of the bed in our bedroom. While applying lavender moisturizing lotion to my skin, I reminisced about my relationship with my daughter. How did I misread our mother- daughter bond? I thought Patsy shared the good and bad in her life with me. How long have I been disillusioned about her life? The long bubble bath hadn't helped prevent me from worrying about her. I was no calmer.

While I continued to lotion myself and still not feeling at peace, I realized I needed the unconditional love a parent could give, so I called my father, Robert Hugo West. He would know what to do.

The phone rang twice before Daddy picked up.

"Daddy! Bounce beat Patsy," I yelped into the phone.

"Oh," my father answered . . . a little too casually.

Huh? My father is known to be countless things. But nonchalant isn't one of them.

"Did you hear what I said, Daddy? Bounce hit Patsy with his fists."

"I heard you," he grumbled as though I was interrupting his day.

I slapped the bed, and the thick lotion flew from my hands

onto my bathrobe. My voice didn't mask my anger and confusion. "Why don't you sound shocked? Did you know he's been punching Patsy?" As close as they were, his casual reaction didn't make sense.

With the phone at my ear still talking to Daddy, I forgot about the lotion on my hands and my half-lotioned legs and wandered into the kitchen. "I knew," he answered. "Didn't you?"

Rage soared through my quaking body. Carolyn knew. Daddy knew. Who else knew? Everyone except me?

"Wait," I yelled, "You *knew* what Bounce was doing, and you didn't do anything about it? That doesn't make sense."

My body tensed while pacing the kitchen floor. I tightened my robe with shaky hands and a racing heart. Before I realized it, I picked up a glass from the dish drainer, slammed it against the wall, and unconsciously paced through the shattered pieces. Blood seeped from my feet to the floor as I railed at my father.

Seeing my blood calmed me.

"I thought you'd be the one to put anyone in a grave for putting hands on your precious granddaughter Patsy. You never allowed me to chastise her in your presence. What are you going to do about it now? Are you going to shoot that man?"

"I'm not doing anything," Daddy said. "Patsy probably provoked him."

"*Excuse* me?" I hissed. "*She* provoked *him*? Is *that* what you said? And what if she did? That doesn't give him the right to beat her like a man." I stopped to take a breath. "My daughter is in the hospital, broken, battered, and bruised. You taught me never to allow a man to disrespect me, let alone physically or mentally abuse me. For God's sake, this is your *granddaughter*, *not* some stranger off the street."

Daddy sighed as though I was emotional over nothing. "Trish, Patsy has a temper. She has *your* temper, and I'm not talking about just during one of her episodes. I've seen her and Bounce go at it countless times. I've witnessed Patsy repeatedly in his face. A man can only take so much before he retaliates."

"The two of them going at it, with one or two bumps and scratches, is one thing," I explained to my daddy. "Even a minor scuffle would've been different than a total beat down."

"Listen, Trish," Daddy said, "I witnessed Patsy fighting Bounce like she had the strength of a full-grown man. She hit him with her fist in the groin, and he grabbed her arm and threw her to the ground. Then while on the ground, she kicked him and knocked him to the ground. It was hard to watch, but he had to defend himself."

"I'm trying to understand why you feel like she deserved it. But still, Daddy, Bounce had no business physically abusing her to the point of hospitalization—Patsy, or any woman, for that matter. No man does." There was silence on the other end of the phone. "He could have just done enough to stop her. And since no man in her life will stand up, he will answer to me."

I could not agree with my father about Patsy and Bounce's physical relationship. Hearing Daddy's assessment was like a knife sunk into my chest. Why would he say such a thing when his granddaughter was lying unrecognizable in a hospital bed?

As I stood there in my kitchen with tears streaming down my face and blood seeping from my feet, I knew our father-daughter relationship would never be the same.

My respect for my daddy faded like the last glimpse of the sun before it disappeared behind the evening clouds. Without saying goodbye, I hung up on him before screaming at the top of my lungs as I crumbled to the floor.

"Ahhh!" Rolling and moaning on the floor, I loudly cried to the Lord, "No daddy, a daughter in the hospital, and a son I don't know if he's good out there on some mission for the government or not. Jesus!"

Malcolm burst into the room. "What's wrong, Trish? What's got you riled up now?"

"Daddy knew about Bounce physically abusing Patsy," I shouted.

Seeing Malcolm standing there speechless, I channeled my anger toward him. "Tell me why *you* aren't angrier about this situation. Do you condone it, just like my daddy?"

I was livid. Didn't *anyone* care anymore about physical abuse? I jumped up, looked Malcolm in the face with a low, cracking voice, and said, "If you ever dream of putting your hands on me in anger, you better kill me." Malcolm stepped away from me as though I had grown two heads.

I stayed my hand in the air. "If not, when you sleep, I'll tie you to the bedposts, pour molasses on your chest, followed by hot grits, and then lye. Then after you die, I'll report it. But I don't expect any jail time. You'll be just another Black wife beater put out of a woman's misery."

Malcolm shook his head. "Trisha, you need to pray and talk to God about this situation. Baby, you don't even realize what you're saying. Look at your feet. They're bleeding. Let me get this glass up and tend to your feet," he pleaded.

"No. I need to find Bounce so I can take care of him since no one else plans to take him out. God has nothing to do with this. Since the men in this family don't have enough backbone to handle this situation, I'll handle Bounce myself," I bellowed.

Wiping my hands, I found my phone and redialed Bounce. Because I'd called him continuously since Patsy's hospitalization, I'd memorized every word of his outgoing greeting. When he didn't answer, I left him a nasty voicemail.

"I will find you," I warned him. "And when I do, I'm going to shoot you. I'm going to kill you. As God is my witness, if I ever see you again, you're a dead man!" And I meant every word I said.

While still shaking with anger, I finally realized my feet were bleeding. Malcolm tried to help, but I pushed him away and tended to my feet while he swept up the glass. Donning my nightgown, I realized Malcolm had also cleaned up the broken mirror.

I shook with rage, and the Holy Spirit tried to reason with the hurt flaming inside me, but I couldn't move past it. At that moment, I understood mental illness. I wanted the crazy to stop, but I couldn't hold it back. I was on a runaway train of anger and vengeance.

Finally getting into bed beside Malcolm, I told him, "It's going to be a long, sleepless night in Georgia."

CHAPTER FIVE

The following morning, I left home early to be at the hospital as soon as visiting hours were allowed. After checking in at the nurse's station, I hurried down the septic-smelling hospital hall to Patsy's room, eager to talk to her. The day before, the doctors had sedated her, and I could only hold her hand, and whisper prayers mingled with rage over her.

I was relieved to see her peeping through her black and blue swollen eyes when I slowly entered the room. "You're awake," I said emotionally. "How are you feeling, baby girl?"

Patsy groaned. Her puffy purple lips scared me. "I feel like I look," she mumbled somewhat incoherently.

After straining to hear, I understood her to say, "Like death warmed over."

While gaping at her, my heart sank. "Have you heard from him," I gently asked.

"No," Patsy answered with a gravelly voice. Finding the only chair in the room, I dragged it to her bed, gently taking Patsy's hand in mine.

"Do you have any idea where he is?"

"No." Patsy turned her face away from me, showing she wasn't in the mood to discuss Bounce. But I had to push her for answers if I wanted to bring him to justice. "Are you pressing charges against him?"

Patsy hesitated for a moment, then whispered, "No."

I exhaled.

"Why not, Patsy? He deserves to go to jail for doing this to you. Actually, he deserves to be in the cemetery, but I'll settle for a jail cell." I didn't reveal my plan to kill Bounce. I didn't want to add additional stress to her already fragile mind and body.

"Mama . . ." After turning to face me, Patsy rolled her eyes at me. Me, the one who was there for her.

"Why didn't you tell me Bounce has been hurting you?"

Patsy winced. "We hurt each other, Mom. Besides, I've taken you through more than enough already. I didn't want to put anything else on you."

I rested my hand over her heart. "I'm your *mother*, baby. That's what I'm here for. To help carry the load when you can't do it alone. Have you forgotten that?"

"Remembering that keeps me, Mama," Patsy whined.

I caressed her swollen face, careful not to hurt her. "You've been through so much; you don't deserve this. A husband's supposed to protect you, not hurt you. When I walked in here and saw you lying here like this . . ."

Tears welled in Patsy's eyes without falling. "It's okay, Mama."

"No, it's *not* okay. And if I ever see Bounce again, I will kill him."

"Don't say that, please!" she whimpered.

"I mean it." Becoming angry, I let my guard down about killing Bounce.

Listening to what I said about Bounce, Patsy became so

agitated her body shook as tears streamed down her face. She began to struggle to catch her breath. I was alarmed that she was having a panic attack as her body heaved, lifting her off the bed. Panicking, I pushed her call button several times in succession.

"Nurse, Nurse!" I called as I ran to the door.

The nurse hurried through the door and when she saw Patsy's agitation, she administered a sedative.

Feeling guilty, I refrained from talking about hurting Bounce when Patsy awakened. I didn't want to keep upsetting her like earlier. Instead, I sat with her most of the day while she spent much of the time dozing on and off.

I kept envisioning killing Bounce in the most elaborate ways.

In the days of our marriage, Malcolm had shared what some would consider macabre pillow talk. But it was bonding for us lovers wanting to share our innermost thoughts with each other. Malcolm shared the five ways he knew to kill a man. It was part of his military training, and believe it or not, it assured me that my husband, who would be away from me for months in places I couldn't pronounce, would know how to protect himself. But the five lessons never left my catalog of what I thought over time was placed in my "useless information" knowledge file. Now, the lessons were linked to "Five Ways to Murder Your Son-in-Law." Or maybe, "How to *Bounce* Someone Out."

I plotted between Patsy's slumber, and each plan was more detailed than the last.

The simplest way was to shoot Bounce directly in the heart. But that wasn't appealing to me. I looked at my baby all broken and bruised, and I wanted him to experience equal pain before I put him out of his misery.

Unbeknownst to my husband, with time on my hands, I'd signed up for membership at a gun range when he and I attended a weapons class. I didn't say anything, not wanting him to feel that I thought an older Malcolm could no longer protect me. A man's ego is so important to nurture. So, instead, I kept it quiet, but over time, I became proficient in marksmanship. Call me bad-packing mama.

I gave a slight grin at my own lunacy. Feeling eyes on me, I turned and saw Patsy was awake again.

"Why do you have that creepy grin on your face, Mama?" she slurred.

Humming, I stroked her arm as gently as possible. "I'm thinking of you when you start to feel better and planning what we will do when you come home."

Whimpering, she fell back asleep, but with a calm, satisfied countenance. This time she slept more soundly.

That allowed me to devise a plan for poisoning Bounce. I figured I'd buy a rare poison that would be undetectable during an autopsy. But I didn't know where to purchase such an item without having it traced back to me. I'd check with my best friend for help if I chose this method to kill Bounce.

Interrupting my daydream, I heard, "Mama, why are you still smiling?"

"Because I'm still thinking about how much I love you," I said.

Patsy peered at me in silence. She pointed toward the water jug. I nodded and poured a swallow into a cup. I raised it to her lips and watched her take a difficult sip. When I narrowed my eyes at her pain, she rushed to assure me.

"I'm okay, Mama. Just tired." Patsy then promptly fell back asleep.

After Patsy slept again, I wondered if drowning him would be difficult for me. I recalled reading about killing someone and wrapping the body in chicken wire loaded with bricks. The wire would keep the body from swelling, and bricks would keep it from floating to the water's surface. But of course, this idea was skewed because unless I caught him off guard, I'd never be able to take him down alone. I knew I couldn't allow someone else to participate in my diabolical scheme.

I looked down, expecting Patsy to wake up, but she slept on. Situating myself in the comfy chair, I heard the door open, and the nurse came in.

"How's our patient doing? I won't be long. I just need to administer more medicine and check her vitals."

As I watched the nurse place more medication in Patsy's bag, I couldn't help but ask, "More sedatives? She's already sleeping a lot."

"Let the nurse due her job, Mama." Patsy's wide eyes stared into mine as though she was trying to figure me out.

"The more she rests, the more she heals," the nurse said, continuing to move around the room. She added fresh pillows under Patsy's head and changed the pillowcases. When she saw Patsy shiver, she added a blanket.

Soon, Patsy's eyes blinked, and she drifted off again.

"Don't worry, ma'am, your daughter will be all right. I've seen worse."

Irritated, I snapped. "Well, this is *my* baby. I don't *want* to see anything happen to her that is not loving and nurturing. I could care less about what others have survived."

"Oh no, ma'am. I didn't mean it like that," the nurse said, her face turning crimson.

"You done?"

Scurrying out of the room, the nurse didn't reply. She just left.

Way to go, girl. Antagonize the people responsible for keeping your child well.

I shook my head at my own gall and hummed, trying to work myself back to my daydream of killing Bounce, lesson number three. That made me smile again.

"Mama, you're still humming and smiling. I must have been asleep for only a minute or two. The nurse left?"

"Yes, and like she said, it's OK to sleep because you need your rest to heal, and I'm here with my mind on you and your release."

Patsy drifted off again before I could even complete my sentence.

Um, I could stab him in the heart. I must have fallen asleep with the hospital channel on an old western because the next thing I knew, I was in a saloon in a western town. The saloon was full of cowboys, and I wore a school marm dress. I rushed up to Bounce dressed like a dime-store villain in a black ten-gallon hat. I pulled my Bowie knife out of my satchel and stabbed him in the heart.

I woke up giggling at this one. Imaging Bounce's demise seemed therapeutic.

But then Patsy cleared her throat. Startled, I slowly turned and gave her an Oscar-winning look of innocence. "Um, happy, sweetie. Sorry, I must have dozed off."

"Uh-uh, what's really going on, Mama? You were giggling."

At this point, I understood I didn't have to answer—just stall her—because Patsy would be asleep again in five minutes. I honestly didn't think she remembered all the times she was in and out of consciousness. Her body was signaling to her it needed rest to heal. And each time she fell asleep, I fell into daydreaming about Bounce's untimely end.

Shortly after stalling Patsy, I could hear her labored breathing. I frowned as I watched the rising and falling of her chest as she slept. Then I envisioned hanging Bounce. But the how-to was escaping me. I'm five feet in my stocking feet, trying to hang a six-foot muscular man over a nine-foot beam in the ceiling of my attic. Although the image of him as "hanging fruit" was quite satisfying, I realized I could not pull off hanging him from a beam.

Although all the scenarios were satisfying, I realized they were also far- fetched. With no one to give Bounce the beat down, poison, drowning, stabbing, or hanging he deserved, I'd have to settle for shooting him.

I thought about purchasing a silver bullet. It would be a nice touch. I saw the headlines now: *"Beware of Silver Bullet Killer!"* Now that I finally had decided on the way, I needed to determine the how. How would I dispose of the body? How would I create my alibi? My head started to hurt as I created scenarios that were soon discarded. I was not a villain and could not perfect a plausible way to take care of Bounce without getting caught. And then it hit me as I continued to plot. I didn't care if I got caught. Seeing the pain on Bounce's face when he realized I'd shot him would be worth it. When the nurse returned from her evening rounds, Patsy woke up. "Patsy, I'll administer your next dose of pain meds. It won't be long before you're asleep again," the nurse advised.

Patsy groaned. "All right. But it seems like it's all I'm doing. I'm sleeping, and for some reason, my mom's either smiling or giggling. Does this medicine make you hallucinate?"

The nurse looked at Patsy, then me. "No, I haven't heard of those side effects. But know that your body knows what it needs to heal."

I flashed a contented smile. "That's exactly what I said, and I'm smiling because I know God is in control," I said as I softly stroked Patsy's hand. I then turned to the nurse. "Thank you for taking such loving care of my daughter. As soon as she sleeps again, I'll tiptoe out."

The nurse filled the tubes in Patsy's arms with the next dose of liquid medication for the pain, then gave her a shot in the stomach to prevent blood clotting. Patsy drifted off as soon as the nurse was out of the room, and I'm sure before she returned to her nurse's station.

Watching the drugs drip into Patsy's body, I prayed that she wouldn't become addicted. Since her drug tolerance has always been low, it would be easy for her to begin to depend on the drugs to keep calm.

Ruminating over what *could* happen, my cell chimed. I kissed Patsy's hand, left the room, then hit answer on the screen.

"Did you check for my messages?" Malcolm asked without me saying hello.

"I'm still at the hospital, and service was bad inside the

room," I explained. "Let me read them now."

"No need. I can tell you. Bounce came by here."

My heart skipped a beat. "For what?"

"He went by Carolyn's and dropped off the kids."

I rushed behind an elderly woman onto the elevator.

"Did you get him?" I yelled, making the woman jump. "Did you shoot him? Please tell me you took care of him." The elevator reached the lobby on the bottom floor, and the poor lady bolted off. "Did you at least give him a beat down?" I wailed.

"In front of the kids, Trish? Listen to yourself. You're better than that." Malcolm didn't hide the agitation coating his voice. "I said what I could without letting the kids know what he did to their mother. And it needs to stay that way."

Not feeling the least bit sorry, but not wanting to agitate Malcolm more, I did lower my voice. "Where'd he go?"

Malcolm exhaled as though he had been holding his breath. "Baby, I don't know. All I know is he's gone. Hopefully, for good. I'll see you when you get home," he said with a strained voice. "I pray God's protection over all of us."

Moving quickly through the lobby, then the parking lot, I got to my car and tried breathing exercises to steady my nerves. Bounce was now number one with a bullet on the lengthy list of people I could never forgive, right behind my evil mother.

Shaking my trembling hands, I started the car and turned to a gospel jazz music station. I needed a minute before making my next move, and music usually calmed me down. And I *needed* to calm down because my mother appeared every time my stress level increased. Sally West was the reason for my mixed-up childhood. The music wasn't doing it because before I could pull off, the screenplay of my childhood streamed through my consciousness.

To others, she was a lovely Christian lady who had my five siblings and me in church every Sunday. She always ensured we wore the prettiest dresses and our hair was neat and freshly done every Saturday night before church. She made sure our bellies were full, a roof was over our heads, and we had clothes on our backs . . . but none of that could erase the abuse we endured. Behind closed doors, my mother was a mean, nasty, child-abusing drunk.

Nothing we did was ever good enough for her. Outside of church, she called us every sordid name except for a child of God. She hit us for no reason and often stumbled into bed while we were sleeping and threw up all over us. She was always a mean, senseless drunk. Because after making the mess, she'd beat us for soiling the bed. My mom branded us with the words, "You're all worthless and can't do anything right."

Nothing ever pleased her; we were never enough for her. Once when I was twelve, Mom cut off my pigtails. All because I drank the last bit of milk. It was like a light went out in her when she did that, and from that day forward, she always picked on me. When I started my period, she was in one of her moods and refused to give me a pad, so I ended up having to wear a sock between my legs. Imagine my embarrassment at school when it fell out in the girls' bathroom. I cringe even now, remembering my humiliation.

I met Malcolm when I was sixteen, and he was eighteen. I fell in love with him immediately and we became intimate right away. My mother was so mean that I got pregnant on purpose. That was my pass for my parents to sign the papers clearing me to get married. That's how desperate I was to get away from her.

After Patsy was born, Malcolm joined the military and we were gone. By the time I turned eighteen, I was a wife and mother on the other side of the world, far away from Mom. And I was happier than I'd ever been before.

Not only could I not stand my mother, but I also didn't trust her. And I never forgave her. When she died years ago, Malcolm forced me to attend her funeral. How do you pay respect to a person you lost respect for a long time ago? Seeing her lying in the casket, I wanted to yell, "Devil in a blue dress!" but I contained myself. After the viewing, I serenely strolled to my seat, grateful her reign of terror was over.

Nevertheless, I always vowed to be a better mother than she was to me. And I tried. God knows I tried.

I sat in the hospital parking lot for an hour before finally pulling off and driving home. When I got there, my grandbabies ran and hugged me as soon as I was inside the house. They were my joy, even if they lived in a household that held more pain than I hoped they'd ever realize. I was glad that Bounce dropped them off.

Malcolm watched from the archway as small arms clutched me and pressed close for some grandmother love. When they had their fill, his eyes caught mine. And as he moved toward me, the compassion that flowed from him to me was a current that flooded my being. He walked with determined and measured steps across the living room and encircled me in a tight squeeze. I exhaled a breath I didn't know I was holding in the safety of his arms.

Looking around him, I saw that the kids had gone into their room to play. With his arm around me, we moved toward the kitchen. I wanted to discuss the day as he saw it. When we first got to the hospital, I was overwhelmed by Patsy's appearance, so I left the room to pull myself together for a while. I never heard what went on when I was out of the room.

"Did Patsy say anything to you when I was out of the room?" I asked.

"No," he said. "And I got so emotional over seeing her like that I couldn't do anything but hold it together until you came back." Then Malcolm surprised me by saying, "I want you to know, I intimately know how you feel. I so wanted to attack Bounce the moment I saw him. But, baby, I had to let the Holy Spirit have governance over me so our grandchildren wouldn't witness me laying these hands on their father."

Malcolm held his large hands in the air in supplication. I hugged him back as tightly as he had done for me moments before. When I pulled away, I felt the powerful emotion surging through his tense body and the stress lines etched across his forehead.

"You good?" I murmured, knowing I had unfairly misjudged his mastery of his emotions.

His eyes were downcast, like his heart was sinking. He was slow to answer but finally said with resolution, "We gon' be all right. We just *gotta* keep praying."

I fought his temperance, rolling my eyes. But I stayed silent. No sense in getting upset with Malcolm and fighting two battles on two fronts. I knew he was trying not to do what his heart wanted him to do. His pre- saved self would have already administered a good old-fashioned beat down, followed by a bullet to Bounce's head. But I extolled the virtues of my saved husband, and I knew it was wrong for me to want him to be something different now. But somebody said it right, "The heart wants what the heart wants."

Later that night, after we put the kids to bed and we snuggled together, the damn broke. Malcolm cried, and with tears streaming down his face, he told me how he wanted to cause bodily harm to Bounce. Although Patsy was now a grown-up, she was still his daughter and he had failed in his responsibility to take care of her. He failed her as a father.

The next morning, the kids woke up with renewed exuberance. "Grandma, Grandma!" The kids circled me to determine if I had had any goodies for them. It was a good thing that I had stopped at the grocery store after Malcolm told me they were at the house the night before.

"Good morning, Grandma's sweeties!" I kissed all three of their foreheads.

"Morning, Grandma," Sophie said. She was nine but mature for her age. Her wide grin revealed the missing teeth knocked out when she fell from a swing while at the playground at school last year. It didn't take away from her being adorable, though.

Hugging me, William said, "Morning, Grandma." He was six and full of joy. He was tall for his age and there wasn't a mean bone in his body. Although the youngest, he helped his sisters with their chores and was the first to hug his mother when he thought she needed one.

Finally, with a quick side hug, Paige said, "Sit down and rest, Grandma. I'm helping with homework they didn't do yesterday and I gave them cereal."

Paige was going on fourteen and had practice helping with her siblings. She reminded me of Patsy the most. She was a pistol, always ready to go off. They were so much alike. I prayed she'd never develop Patsy's issues. Since bipolar disorders manifested during the young adult life stage, I still had years to pray for her mental wellness. I needed to pray for the mental health of each of my grandchildren. The family generational curse of mental illness could appear at any time in any or all three of them. I was constantly on the lookout for symptoms.

When I look back on it, Patsy's decision to have children was a big surprise. She *never* liked kids. Babysitting was out of the question during her teenage years. Patsy preferred to work at McDonald's rather than take care of children. She tolerated her younger brother only because she had to, despite us promoting love in our household. After living with my mother, showing love was my golden rule. Malcolm and I took the kids to amusement parks and other small weekend getaways as often as possible. We enjoyed spending time with them. Our son—Malcolm Jr.—was in the military and had no children yet, so we spoiled Patsy's.

Malcolm joined us in the kitchen. "Grandpa!" the kids exclaimed as they raced from the kitchen chairs to their hero.

I watched as Paige was last to hug him but hugged him the longest. I would need to reevaluate whether all the kids really didn't know what had happened to Patsy. At Paige's age and astuteness, she could very well have witnessed and understood more than we thought she did.

"Paige has already given the kids their breakfast and is then going to help them with their homework," I told Malcolm, staring at him hard to let him know there was more going on here.

But Malcolm either chose not to respond to my prompting or really didn't catch it because he gave Paige a huge smile and said, "That's my girl. Always so helpful."

Clearing my throat, I sat at the table, and the kids sat around it, joyfully going back to slurping their cereal. I felt Malcolm at my back, squeezing my shoulders gently. This time, I cleared my throat again, but louder. Stopping in a mid-spoon shovel, three pairs of eyes looked at me. When Paige put her spoon down, they followed.

"Babies, your mother is in the hospital, and while she is getting better, it will be a while before you can see her," I said, keeping my voice soft and calm.

His eyes welling with tears, my baby boy, William, who tells all he feels, said, "Is my mama okay, Grandma?"

Before I could answer, Paige said sullenly. "Mama's all right. Eat your cereal, William."

Malcolm squeezed my shoulders again, indicating that he heard what I heard. Paige was mad. She was angry at either Patsy, Bounce, or probably both. She picked up her spoon and slurped her cereal into her mouth. Sophie and William picked up their spoons and did the same as their big sister. Their actions said clearly to me, "If Paige said the conversation is over, it's over."

I rose, feeling dejected. Bounce had so much to answer for, and I had so much work in front of me.

Shaking off my melancholy, I said, "Guys, when you finish your breakfast and homework, I've got some things for you."

I went over to the bag of items I had bought and placed in a chair the night before, reached in, and handed the kids a bubble- making kit. They cheered and then began to rush through their breakfasts, clamoring to Paige that they wanted to finish their homework quickly.

Noting they were all busy, I pulled my phone out of my pocket and marched into the family room. I phoned the hospital and spoke to the nurse's station.

They stated that while Patsy was still in pain, she appeared to rest more comfortably and had registered her pain at a seven instead of a nine.

Frown lines appeared around the ridges of my forehead. Malcolm leaned over and began to use his finger to stroke them gently as though he could erase them. I quietly thanked the nurse and said I would be there in a while.

"Is she better today?" he whispered. At that moment, I realized the tenseness of his body and tight fist exuded his controlled anger.

"Take a wild guess," I snapped. There I was, getting angry at Malcolm again for what Bounce did. I recognized my misplaced anger, but it seemed unavoidable.

"Is Mama sick again?" Sophie asked. Malcolm and I didn't know she was outside the door, eavesdropping on our conversation. By then, Paige and William had eased down the hallway and joined Sophie, listening to Malcolm's and my discussion.

I cringed. The older Sophie got, the harder it was to hide things from her. And if Sophie had a clue, Paige knowing all was a no-brainer. "Mama will be all better soon, okay? Now, how about Grandma cook your favorite meal for dinner tonight?"

"Yay!" The kids jumped for joy. Paige gave me a significant nod and then got all of them settled in the family room.

I headed to the kitchen to take some meat out of the freezer. Malcolm followed closely behind.

"I still feel like you should've at least knocked him out," I growled under my breath as I stuck my head in the freezer.

Whispering, Malcolm's sighed, "Can we not right now? We shouldn't be discussing this anywhere near the kids. I think they know enough already."

"Yes, I think you're right. William is probably the only one who doesn't understand." I lowered my voice. "But just thinking about it gets me riled up all over again. You saw the way Patsy's face looked. How could you not knock his teeth out, Malcolm? At least the nurse says she's having a better day today."

Malcolm took me in his arms and muttered, "Things have a way of working out for the best. The Holy Spirit will find a way to handle Bounce without you becoming involved."

My shoulders slumped like a pin stuck in me, and all the air escaped into the room. "Things won't be okay until Bounce is six feet under."

My cell rang, interrupting us. "Hello?" I answered the phone and tucked it between my chin and shoulder as I ran water over the frozen meat.

A polite, professional voice filled the air. "This is Beatrice from Emory Hospital. We just wanted to inform you that we returned to the room to check on your daughter and found her gone. As her official contact person, we felt you should know this was against her doctor's orders."

The nozzle on the faucet slipped from my hand, and water sprayed me in my face. Gasping, I yelled, then looking down the hallway to make sure the kids didn't hear me, lowered my voice, and said, "Gone? What do you mean, gone?"

"Ma'am, she's not here. I can see by your reaction she didn't leave with you."

My heart raced. What was this child doing? "I just talked to your staff thirty minutes ago and was told she was fine. What are you people doing up there?" I whispered furiously. "No, she's not with me."

There was silence on the other end. Then a very stilted voice replied, "Okay, ma'am. We will call you back if anything changes on this end." She then abruptly hung up on me.

"What's happened?" Malcolm rushed over to me.

"It's Patsy."

Malcolm grimaced and rubbed his hands down his face. "Is she okay?"

I shook my head, bleakness stamped across my face. "I don't know. The hospital just called, saying she's not in her room. She's gone, Malcolm!" For the second time since this ordeal began, Malcolm's emotions broke. His body trembled as his face became a river of water. "Gone where?" he stuttered.

Light-headed, I slowly backed into a bar stool at the counter and sat down. "I don't know. Oh, Lord, please let Patsy be all right. Please help us locate her before she has an episode."

When I looked up, Paige stood in the archway, but she turned and walked back down the hallway before I could speak.

CHAPTER SIX

After spending a week of sleepless nights worrying about Patsy, I called Carolyn and told her about my inability to sleep. When Malcolm decided to take the kids out for the afternoon, I invited her over for a visit, telling her my listlessness from lack of sleep was overwhelming.

Although I was still peeved with Carolyn about Patsy, I needed my best friend.

I waited for Carolyn on the front porch. When she arrived, I invited her to sit in the living room with me. Before sitting, she squinted and leaned into me, noticing the dark circles around my swollen eyes.

Then remembering that I experienced nightmares when stressed, she said, "Trish, you need to see someone about those bad dreams."

I glanced away to avoid her probing glare. "I'll be fine," I lied.

Carolyn shook her long, silver tresses away from her flawless face. Her light brown complexion flushed pink—a sign of the oncoming tirade I didn't want to hear. Our friendship sometimes surprised me. We were complete opposites and rarely agreed on most topics, but I could always depend on

Carolyn whenever I needed her. She and Malcolm consistently held me up.

"You're not fine," she fussed in her thick Southern drawl. "The sooner you stop lying to yourself, the better."

My bottom lip quivered. "It's been a week since anyone has seen or heard from Patsy. I've repeatedly called her, but her phone goes straight to voicemail. I've contacted every hospital in Georgia other than Emory, as well as the jails and the morgues. No one has a record of her being at any of them. Patsy is not missing. She's hiding—doesn't want to be found. And a 'don't want to be found Patsy' is an 'absent Patsy.'"

Carolyn leaned in and hugged me so firmly that I had to catch my breath. "She's with Bounce. I can feel it in my bones."

"Despite what he did to her, I know that's where she is," I whimpered into Carolyn's shoulder. "A mother always knows."

I then admitted I had sunk to reaching out to the man I currently hated with my entire being.

"Bounce isn't answering my calls or responding to my text messages either." With a sigh, I massaged my temples. "I've passed Patsy and Bounce's house a hundred times in the past week, praying that Patsy's okay, but nobody's been there."

Carolyn snorted. "You're going to be stuck raising these kids," she said dryly.

Stung by her callousness, I scooted away. "They're my grandbabies, Carolyn. I'm not 'stuck' doing anything because I love them. I'd rather have those children here with me than with either of those fools they call parents."

Carolyn shrugged. "I'm just saying."

"Listen, having my grandbabies here with me hasn't been so bad," I tried to explain, "Paige helps me with the younger ones. She's very mature for her age and sassy, just like her mama. She's more helpful than Patsy was at that age, though."

I couldn't help but chuckle, comparing the two of them. "Patsy was as lazy as a snail on a log and never wanted to do anything. She barely ventured outside as a child because she didn't want to get hot or dirty. That girl could sit up in her messy room all day long without cleaning it. I never quite understood that about her."

"Patsy's always been different. A solitary soul," Carolyn murmured. "It's part of the reason Bounce could abuse her for so long without me knowing. It started way before Patsy told me. I'm thankful I was available when she couldn't hold it in anymore."

My brows rose. I was still uncomfortable that Patsy went to everyone except her father or me. I waved my hand to move on from the subject. "Enough about me and my problems. Let's talk about you and Deacon Smith. You said in our last phone conversation that he may become an issue for you."

"Chile," Carolyn smiled, "Deacon Smith is about to make me sin."

"Carolyn!"

"What? I've got needs, you know. And the way he looked last Sunday in that beige and brown pinstriped suit . . ." Carolyn shimmied and fanned herself like she was hot. "I'm trying to see what's underneath all those nice clothes."

"You better repent, girl." I tossed my head back and laughed. "He's a *deacon*. Yield not to temptation. Hands off until you marry him."

"No promises. I'm not *that* saved. If he's down for a little sinning, then I'm all in." Carolyn rose in her seat and twerked for effect.

I hollered, needing that spot of comic relief in my life.

Carolyn could always get me there.

I hesitated but needed to share a sin I hadn't even told Malcolm. "Okay, Video Mama. I've wanted to sin myself."

Carolyn rubbed her hands together. "Girl, tell me all the juicy details."

"I swear I've wanted to drink an entire bottle of wine these days to take me out of this mood I'm experiencing. I just want to be numb, you know? Then I can handle focusing on my daughter." Admitting that aloud made me feel ashamed.

"You can have a drink or two without losing your salvation, Trish," Carolyn assured me with sympathetic eyes. "If it'll help take the edge off or stop the nightmares, do you. I think sometimes we can get caught up in the shame and forget we're human in the midst of our striving for divinity."

I twisted my hands with a groan. "Every night, I dream about Patsy. Each dream has horrendous acts happening to her. Last night, I dreamed she was sitting alone in the dark, in her hospital gown barefoot—on the edge of a cliff. Her skin was as cold as ice. The purple color of her lips was like the injuries under her eyes. Her matted hair contained leaves and sticks, like she'd been running through a forest for hours."

"Oh, Trish. I'm so sorry."

In a trancelike motion, I continued. "Patsy sat there, crying, praying, and talking to herself about her problems. She kept asking herself why she was born crazy. Said she was tired of the fight for normalcy. Then she jumped while I watched. That's when I woke up."

Carolyn gasped. "Jesus, Trish, I wouldn't sleep, either. That's why you look so exhausted." She touched the bags underneath my eyes.

I knew I looked terrible, but I was tired of it all. I didn't want to think about it anymore. "Shut up, girl. I'm forty-eight and still as fine as wine. Malcolm says I still got it. It's all alright with him, more cushion for the . . ." I patted my hips to finish the sentence. Carolyn and I laughed together.

"All jokes aside, Patsy's going to be okay. She's going to come home, Trish. She always does," Carolyn said.

Patsy's episodes had been whirlwinds over the years. First, she refused to go to the hospital, disappearing for days. But eventually, she always returned to us.

Day after day, there would be no word from Patsy. So, Malcolm and I spent days sitting by the phone waiting for news about her, even calling the local hospitals and morgues periodically.

After placing APBs out on her, the police finally asked us to exhaust all avenues to locate her before reporting her missing again. Her history of disappearing and reappearing forced our compliance with the police's request. We did all we could while waiting until she returned home in a better mood than when she left. Patsy acted as though there were no problems. And there weren't . . . until there were, again.

In the end, however, Patsy had no choice. It had gotten too far out of hand. She'd reached the point where she agreed to go to the hospital for an evaluation. Unfortunately, they diagnosed her with dissociative identity disorder and bipolar disorder.

Malcolm and I were devastated. And my guilt mounted. My family history is rearing its ugly head on my little girl.

But at least now we knew what was wrong with her. Although the literature didn't support mental illness having a genetic link with family members, I believed that mental illness could be hereditary. Hence, my guilt. Growing up, besides my mother, I had additional people with mental illness in my family, but my uncle Bingo was the one I remember the most.

Unfortunately, during my childhood, there was no name for it. The old folks used to say my uncle was a little "touched" or had the devil in him, but now I know he was sick. Some days he was serene, on others he'd turn into an erratic, uncontrollable, and mean man none of us recognized. I avoided him and would run if I saw him coming. His multiple personalities frightened me, especially when he called me in different voices.

"Trisha, Trisha!" Bingo taunted, sounding like a monster. "Come help me, Trisha," he begged like a baby girl. Watching my daughter go through the same thing wasn't as scary as it was back then. It was sad and hurt me that I couldn't do more for her. I wished I could give my uncle Bingo the compassion I was too ignorant to know he needed when I was younger.

"Trish? Trish!" Carolyn snapped her fingers in my face.
"Were you talking to me?"
"I told you I'm going home to cook dinner." She looked concerned. "Where'd you go to? You were so far gone."
"Just traipsing down memory lane."
Although I invited Carolyn over and was happy to see her, I was ready for her to hit the road. "Thanks for coming. I'll keep you posted."

I walked Carolyn to the door and stepped out onto the porch with her. The cool wind brushed my face, so I sat for a spell.

Carolyn sniffed the sweet fragrance coming from my flower bed on her way out. Admiring the mix of roses and daisies on the porch, Carolyn asked if she could join me to enjoy the sweet fragrance of the flowers. "Well, maybe for a minute," I said.

After rocking together in solitude for a minute or two, a car pulled into our driveway.

"MJ!" Standing from my chair, I flashed my first genuine smile in days.

Malcolm Jr. hopped out of the car and came toward us with the confident stride learned from the stern discipline taught in the military. He was stationed six hours away in Fayetteville, NC.

"Hey, Mama!" he exclaimed when he reached me.

"Aw, my baby!" I embraced my boy, full of pride. He may have followed in his father's footsteps, but our son was a lot like me—not physically because he was tall, dark, and handsome. But his keen intelligence, loving nature, and helpful demeanor were all mine. And we both burned in the kitchen. We loved feeding people.

Giving me a once-over, MJ kissed my cheek and enthusiastically lifted me from my feet, "I missed you, Mama."

Realizing he must see the circles around my eyes, I said, "I missed you too, son, and I'm fine. I really am."

Nodding to me, he turned, "Hi, Ms. Carolyn." He then stepped over to her and gave her a sweet hug.

"Hey, MJ!" Carolyn grinned widely. "Looking good, son. How old are you again?"

I popped her hands. "Hands off, Carolyn. He's too young for you."

Carolyn raised both her hands in the air. "What'd I say?"

MJ ignored Carolyn's antics with a chuckle. "Have you heard from Patsy yet?"

"No, son."

"What about Bounce?" His smile disintegrated into a frown. "I've got a bone to pick with him. Nah, let me be clearer.

I'm going to whoop him worse than he did to my sister."

"It's okay. I'm glad to hear somebody's as angry as I am," I sighed, relieved. "Your father and grandpa are walking around here like they aren't upset with Bounce at all. It's like they don't care about what he did to Patsy. Well, not your father. He's upset but is allowing God to handle it."

"Well, after I'm done with him, he'll never put his hands on Patsy or any other woman again. I promise you that."

"That's my boy," I smiled. "Go on and get your bags out of the car and take them into the house so you can get settled in. How long are you staying?"

"I'll be here for about a week."

Carolyn waited until MJ rounded up his things and disappeared into the house. "That boy might kill Bounce."

"I wish someone would," I said. "Stop it, Trish."

"Are we acting innocent?" I smirked. "Or did you forget I'm aware of *your* little secret?"

Immediately, Carolyn became visibly uncomfortable. I'd dug up a memory she had worked hard to forget.

"Trish . . ." She sounded wounded. "What?"

Carolyn hurriedly grabbed her purse and prepared to leave.

"Don't go, Carolyn. I didn't mean to bring it up, and I'm sorry. I'll take it to my grave."

Carolyn exhaled. "I've asked for forgiveness for what I did. You don't need to throw it in my face." She spun on her heels, stalked off the porch, and hopped into her car. I felt awful watching her drive away. We all have secrets. I hoped Carolyn knew hers was safe with me.

CHAPTER SEVEN

As Carolyn's car disappeared down the street, Malcolm and the kids pulled into the driveway. After Malcolm helped them from the car, they raced to the porch. Faces stained with ice cream, they ran past me, giggling and waving.

Racing behind them, Paige said, "Don't worry about cleaning them up, Grandma. I've got them."

Malcolm stopped and bent to kiss my cheek and said, "Paige is growing into quite the young lady. I'm proud of how she helps with the younger ones," he smiled before saying, "I see MJ's here. I'll go on inside to talk to him."

Nodding, I sat back down and continued rocking with a nod.

Sophie bolted back outside. "Hello, sweet pea," I said. "You good?"

"I'm okay, Grandma. I just spoke to Mama."

My heart skipped a beat. "What?" "Mama called the house phone. But since you didn't answer, she told me not to get anyone because she wanted to check on her kiddos. Then she asked how we were doing. I told her we're fine, but we miss her." I slapped my knee and jumped up.

"Yes! She's alive. My Patsy is alive."

Sophie's eyes grew enormous, but she continued explaining. "Mama asked if you and Grandpa were okay, and I said yes. Then she said to tell you not to worry about her and to give you a kiss from her." She stood on her toes, and I bent forward, letting her peck me on the cheek. I struggled to maintain my smile so Sophie couldn't see that I was seriously worried.

"Did she say where she is?"

"No, but she said she's coming home soon."

Sophie turned and skipped into the house, and I trailed behind her into the kitchen to find my phone. When I checked my call log, I wanted to scream. Patsy had called from a private blocked number.

She's definitely with Bounce.

I was familiar with the games people played to run from their parents into the arms of the one they consider a safe harbor. But unfortunately, Patsy failed to realize Bounce was her storm, and a typhoon was coming.

~~~

I sat comfortably on the porch when MJ stepped out of the house and sat beside me, proudly announcing with a smile, "I met someone. Her name is Clara, and she's originally from California." Then puffing out his chest, he happily proclaimed, "I'm in love, Mama."

"Really? Don't you think twenty-four is too young to fall in love?"

"Naw. If I'm old enough to serve and even die for my country, love is the bonus of life." MJ reached over and gave me a one-armed hug. "Mama, I think she's the one."
~~~

Realizing that I was raining on his parade, I changed my deposition. "Really?" I squealed with as much enthusiasm as I could muster.

"Really, Mama. I didn't want to get married until I retired from the military, but Clara's changed my mind. She's the woman for me, the one of my dreams." I could tell from the look in his eyes that MJ was serious. "Then bring her home to me and your dad." I stood and kissed his cheek. "I'm so happy for you."

MJ wanted a dramatic proposal. In planning, he went from an airplane trailing a banner flying through the sky to popping the question on the jumbotron at a basketball game. I wondered where he got that from. Finally, after exhausting the most outlandish ideas, he concluded that since he didn't have enough time to go big, a simple wedding proposal would suffice. He settled on a romantic dinner at a fancy restaurant. He'd have a server put the ring in a glass of wine, then pop the question when Clara found it.

Talking about wedding plans with MJ brought me back to Patsy's wedding day. Refusing to wear a white dress, she entered the chapel wearing a pale yellow, strapless lace gown with one of the longest trains I'd ever seen. Her timeless beauty showed through the glow on her face. At least two hundred individual petite yellow flowers were strung throughout her hair. Her gold earrings were so long they grazed the top of her chest; she opted not to wear a necklace.

Patsy was one of the most beautiful creations I'd ever seen as she stood impatiently at the altar to marry Bounce.

She was so crazy about him and so sure about him. They were so in love. Patsy would call and talk to me about him for hours, sharing all these amazing stories about the fantastic dates and adventures Bounce took her on, like horseback riding and picnicking in the deep woods. But out of all their special dates, their engagement was my favorite.

Bounce made it a day to remember. First, he proposed to Patsy on a television commercial he was filming for one of his dealerships. Then when he proposed and gifted my baby a brand-new Lexus from his lot, the commercial went viral and had a million hits from people. It was beautiful and drove tons of business to Bounce's dealership. I've seen that commercial at least a thousand times.

"Mama?" MJ interrupted my thoughts. "I need to talk to you."

"What is it, son?"

MJ inhaled and then rushed his announcement. "I figured Bounce was hitting her."

"What?! Why did you think that?" My chair rocked back and forth swiftly in agitation.

"Pasty never told me, but I saw them argue awhile back. The way Bounce held her arm, I didn't enjoy seeing the fear on her face. She tried to play it off once she saw me, but I knew she was in trouble. I can't believe I just let her brush it off like nothing. Especially when I saw the bruise on her arm later that day." MJ hung his head.

Reaching across and taking his hand in mine, I commiserated with him. "It's not your fault, son. I've always told you to stay out of married folks' business. You were doing what I taught you to do. But your father and I feel the same way. We too missed the signs."

Scowling while punching one of his fisted hands into the other, MJ said, "I'm out here on the front line fighting to protect people I don't know. Meanwhile, I wasn't around to protect my sister." Shadowboxing, MJ continued, "I'm trained with moves that could take him out, and I know how to do it, where he would never be found again."

I turned my son's face toward me. "Hey, look at me. Don't worry about Patsy." MJ didn't respond, but I searched his eyes and knew he had heard me. I squeezed his chin between my fingers. "Son, you can't end up in prison over this."

Leave Bounce to me. I'll do the time.

Although proud of his accomplishments, I never wanted my son to be in the military. I dreamed of a different life for him, like being a lawyer or doctor. As far as I was concerned, he should've been at home, so I wouldn't have spent hours worrying about him. Not because he was in the military but because MJ's always been so sensitive and wore his heart on his sleeve. As a child, he cared for people and refused to go near toy guns. I just knew war would destroy him.

But in 2008, MJ enlisted in the army to serve in the war with Iraq. He said he wanted to follow in his father's footsteps. He proved me wrong and was an excellent soldier, moving up in rank quickly.

Seeing how upset MJ was about Patsy, I needed to pivot to a lighter conversation.

"Let's discuss this proposal, son. Have you picked out a ring? Do you know what she likes? Let's go to the jewelry store later today. I'll help you choose the perfect ring."

MJ smiled, and I was happy that I could bring joy to at least one of my children's lives.

CHAPTER EIGHT

The next day, I was preparing a big country breakfast for the family. The smells of sizzling bacon, homemade sausage with sawmill gravy, my fluffy homemade biscuits with country ham, scrambled eggs with cheese, buttered grits, shrimp in a rue sauce, salmon patties, fruit, juice, and coffee permeated the house.

Everyone was happy to have this breakfast in honor of MJ coming home. I didn't have to call them to the table. When I put the last dish on the table, the family was ready to take their seats.

Although I was busy preparing the meal, I was still trying to figure out Patsy's whereabouts, so I kept my cell phone nearby to see if she had called me using that number, and I had all calls from the house phone forwarded to mine.

While taking the bacon out of the oven, my phone rang. Throwing the hot pan down, I rushed to answer it. "Hello?"

"Mama?"

After waiting all day and night, desperate for her to call, my heart nearly jumped out of my chest at the sound of Patsy's voice. "Patsy, honey. How are you?" "I'm okay, Mama. How are the kiddos?"

"They miss their mother. Where are you?" My voice strained as I held back the tears burning my eyes.

I could hear Patsy cover the phone and then come back and answer me. "I'll be home soon."

Without preamble, I asked, "Are you with him?"

"No, Mama."

I settled down and lowered my voice. "Are you lying?"

"No, Mama," she said.

"Baby, please come home," I begged. Malcolm appeared in the doorway, staring intensely at me, awaiting my words. "I'll come home soon, Mama. First, I want to get myself together. I want to be better."

I locked my eyes with Malcolm. "I can help you get better, baby."

"No, Mama, you can't, but I love you.Bye."

Before I could say another word, she hung up. I stared at the screen, distraught.

"I can't call her back. She called me from a private number."

"What did she say?" Malcolm asked. "That she's getting better and coming home soon. How long is soon?" I asked. "When is soon?"

Malcolm grabbed and rocked me back and forth. In a soothing voice, he said, "I don't know, baby. She's going to come home when she thinks she's ready. She always has."

Those words reminded me of how often we had been made to wait on Patsy. When you have someone in your family with mental health issues, they are unpredictable, and even the professionals are more wrong than right when dealing with them.

Patsy ran away from home once when she was sixteen. She'd gotten mad at me because I wouldn't let her go to a party and I sent her to her room. When I called her for dinner, I discovered Patsy had climbed out of her bedroom window. She disappeared for three days. I must've gone to the police station at least twenty times for help but they did nothing. Then, on day three, Patsy finally walked through the front door. I was so happy to see her. I hugged her and cried like a baby instead of being angry. I was just glad she was home.

That was the first time I'd ever had to imagine my life without my baby girl.

"I want and need her back," I told Malcolm. "I miss her . . . the *old* Patsy, before the sickness. I want my baby back."

"She's coming back, Trish. But she's coming back as the Patsy she's evolved into. We have to recognize that and have a little faith."

"Faith," I said, "I've always tried to have faith. Singing in the church choir every Sunday, teaching Bible study, paying my tithes, and serving our God. Even though I sometimes fall short, I try to live right and be a good person."

"God is sovereign. This too will turn out as He planned. But, baby, the things you named are the works of faith. You also need to practice the substance of faith. It's built on the hope and evidence of things we can't see," Malcolm said. That was his mantra from sunrise to sunset, and I must admit, it was getting old. "I'm going to order pizza for the kids' dinner."

I grabbed him by the hand before he walked away. When Malcolm looked back at me, I wondered, when was the last time we had been intimate? I couldn't even remember.

We used to have sex regularly . . . until Malcolm had sex with someone else. Yes, three years ago, my perfect Malcolm had an affair. And it was my fault.

Patsy and the kids took up all my time. What time I didn't devote to them, I dedicated to the church. I attended every church event I could, hanging out with the ladies from the insurance agency I worked for and whatever else I found interesting. I was intimate with Malcolm whenever he wanted, but I wasn't giving him the time and attention he craved. Even then, sex amounted to only lazy encounters out of obligation.

Eventually, my husband received the passion he asked of me from another woman willing to give it.

The night I discovered Malcolm's infidelity, I came home and found the house pitch black.

"Malcolm?" I called out, but there was no response. I dug out my cell and called him, but he didn't answer. I hadn't talked to him all day.

Two hours after I went to bed, Malcolm marched into our bedroom and confessed. He told me he'd just come from having sex with another woman and that it had happened twice before.

Stunned, I sat in disbelief, trying to process his confession. I snapped. As I beat his chest, I cried and demanded to know who the other woman was. In the middle of a full- blown rage, I stopped when I realized why Malcolm had come clean: he didn't want to live that way. Instead of having an affair, he was looking for a divorce.

That's when it hit me. I'd been losing my husband for years without realizing it. It was not his fault. I'd become so caught up with Patsy's life that I'd been negligent in my duties as a wife to Malcolm. I put the grandchildren first when they were here, and on countless days, I cooked dinner for them to eat with us or took what I prepared to Patsy's house. And if she wasn't in a good mood when I got there, I spent the night there without bothering to call Malcolm and let him know I was staying the night.

I understood my role in our marital breakdown and listened

to the Holy Spirit telling me that his affair could be forgiven and the marriage made stronger. So, taking heed to words from the Spirit that would always guide me in truth, I forgave Malcolm for the affair and vowed to be a better wife.

And I had been . . . until this incident with Patsy.

Although sex was the last thing on my list of concerns, I needed my husband in every way tonight. I wanted intimacy.

"Make love to me, Malcolm," I whispered.

"Right now? You were just putting breakfast on the table, Trish," he said in a husky voice.

"Whoops! I'll tell you what. Afterthe heavy breakfast I've made, we'll say we need a little nap, and MJ can spend time with the kids."

Malcolm leaned down and added a wet, passionate kiss to my lips. "That's for thinking like a woman who desires her husband. Thank you, baby. This breakfast is about to be inhaled."

Laughing like a schoolgirl, I almost skipped back into the kitchen.

Paige was standing by the oven, taking out the biscuits. "I got it, Grandma."

MJ then called from the table. "We good? 'Cause a man mad hungry."

Exchanging grins, Malcolm and I got to work. He grabbed the platters that were warming and carried them to the center of the table.

Soon, the pleasing sounds of smacking, talking, and giggling filled the room. Malcolm and I exchanged secretive glances as he shoved his food down his throat.

"Whoa, Dad. Slow down," MJ crowed. "You act like this is a race, not a marathon. This food is too good to rush. I'ma take my time."

"Well, young man, you do that. Your daddy has things to do."

I couldn't help it, I chuckled out loud, winking at my husband as though we were both back in our early twenties when life was good and we only had to worry about paying a bill.

I sobered at the thought. Being unable to pay a bill would be a beautiful thing right about now. I'd rather that than the constant heartache of a child who struggled in every area of her life.

Help me, Jesus! We didn't know how good we had it.

Malcolm pushed his plate away from the table. He then stretched loudly and said, "I think I'll take a little nap."

Eyes going up in his head, MJ protested. "Dad, you just said you had things to do."

"Yeah, I need to go take this nap." Before MJ could protest further, William chirped, "I'm done, Grandma."

"Okay, sweetie pie. Take your plate to the counter and wash your hands and face." "Me too, Grandma," Sophie said as she picked up her plate and took it to the counter. Paige put down her fork and patted her stomach. "Grandma, I need to know how to make those biscuits come out so good. Mine taste like bricks."

"Bricks don't taste that bad," Sophie chimed in.

"Uh-uh. Taste like dirt inside of bricks," William added.

"You guys are gonna regret that," Paige said as she laid her plate on the counter and ran after her siblings.

MJ looked sadly down at his plate. "A man should have the

time to have a second and third helping from his coming home breakfast feast, but I see other things of a higher matter are in play here." He stood and took his plate to the sink. He then began to run dishwater. "I got this, Mama. Go on and rest. I'll put the food up too. Might was well get practice for later."

"That's right. Learn to make that woman happy," I said as I moved into the family room and pulled up a movie from my Amazon Prime library that I bought for times like this. "Come here, you guys, and you can watch this movie I got for you."

Sophie ran over and peeked at the television. "Oooh, it's Spiderman. The one who looks like cousin Jace."

Paige looked at the picture on the big screen. "You know, I'm so glad you finally caught on that they are streaming movies now. You don't need videos," she teased, pointing at the old VCR videos lining the shelf.

"I heard you loud and clear the last time you were here. 'Grandma, we've seen all these old videos fifty times.' So, I did something different and got with the times," I chuckled.

I then stretched my arms out wide and yawned. "I think I'm going to lie down for a while too. You guys be good out here. No fighting and no tussling over the remote."

Almost running down the hallway, I slowed down when MJ called after me, "Have a good nap, Mama." Then he laughed like he had just heard the best joke.

I ignored the ribbing and slowly opened my bedroom door. Malcolm came out of our bathroom with a towel around his waist. Running over to him, I wrapped my arms around his neck and said in a sultry voice while pulling him toward our bed, "I started one of their favorite movie series, the newest one. Make love to me. I need to feel you. Help me overcome this feeling of despair. Paige will make sure they're okay. You know she likes to be in charge."

"You don't have to explain." Malcolm gently took my hand and rushed me to our bed. He then went over and locked the door. He lay next to me and devoured my mouth with a kiss.

Malcolm was my first love and soon became my world. My one and only. Before I forgave him, I considered cheating on him to get even for him having an affair. I tried going through with it, but I couldn't do it. The thought of allowing another man to touch, kiss, or give myself to him . . . I just couldn't. And I never would.

Malcolm laid me on my back and brought me into another world without pain or hurt. Just him. Just me. A world of pure bliss. After all these years, sex with my husband was still as good as ever. He knew my body and how to please me.

CHAPTER NINE

Thirty minutes later, I headed to the kitchen and was pleased to see MJ had cleaned it just as he was taught. While I was in the kitchen inspecting MJ's work, Sophie came in and climbed onto the bar stool, swinging her legs that were far from reaching the floor, and asked, "Grandma, do you and Grandpa fight?"

In a puzzled voice, I asked, "What do you mean, honey?"

"Do you and Grandpa fight like Mama and Daddy?"

I took a deep breath. "You saw your parents fighting?"

"Yes," she confirmed. "One time, we were supposed to be in the den watching television or playing video games, but the door was open, and we saw them across the hall in their bedroom. First, I saw Mama slap Daddy; then he pushed her against the wall." "I saw them punching each other like they were in an Avenger's game," William chimed in as he came into the room. "Sometimes, Mama wins, and sometimes, Daddy does when they fight," he explained. "But mostly, Daddy just holds Mama down until she changes into nice Mama. I like nice Mama the best."

"The other mama doesn't like us," Sophie said.

My heart thundered through my chest cavity. What was I hearing my poor babies saying?

Paige then entered the room. "You guys were supposed to be letting Grandma know the movie is buffering," she said, then turned to me. "I couldn't get it to stop."

"Okay, Paige. I'll get it. Do you know what these babies are saying?" I asked, hoping she would say they were mistaken.

Paige exhaled like she was already tired from the telling of it.

"Yes, ma'am. There are two mamas. The nice one we call Patsy. And the mean one we don't call anything. She's the one who doesn't want kids, and she tells us that when she's yelling at us. Even Daddy doesn't like the other mama," Paige said, sitting next to the other two on the kitchen bar stool.

"They're all your mama, Paige," I said, real low. My earlier buzz from being in my husband's arms faded fast.

Paige sucked her bottom lip and folded her arms. "No, ma'am. She told us she wasn't Patsy and don't call her that name. Then when we asked her what to call her, she said nothing. So, we call her 'the other mama.'"

"Dear God," I murmured.

"But Patsy loves us. She cooks and takes care of us. The other mama forgets to cook and sometimes leaves us alone for hours at a time. Now, she no longer has to convince us. We know she is the other mama, and the other mama doesn't want to be a mother."

"I saw them fighting on Christmas," Sophia added, not wanting to be left out. "Mama threw a glass of juice at Daddy, and his head bled. That was a bad one. Then with his head bleeding, Daddy pushed Mama on the floor, and she didn't move, so we helped her get up and go to bed. She made us promise not to tell you, Grandma. When Daddy came back the next day, he took Mama to the hospital. She stayed in the hospital for a long time after that. Remember, Grandma? We stayed with you and Granddad."

"What?" I tried to keep my voice steady, but my body was in an emotional upheaval.

Sophia nodded. "That time, Mama turned into mean Mama. She got in Daddy's face and started fighting and cursing him out. Then she started swinging her arms like this." Sophia swung her arms in a windmill. "Daddy tried to hold her, but she started biting him and calling him all kinds of names. Daddy said she was belligerent, whatever that means. But that's what Daddy says when Mama acts like that."

"Sweet Jesus," I whispered.

Sophia kept talking as though she had so much more to share. "Daddy couldn't hold her down, so he told us to go outside and wait for him. I peeped through the kitchen door window and saw Mama jump on Daddy's back. Then Daddy knocked Mama onto the floor to get her off his back. Mama ends up on the floor a lot. Then Daddy leaned down and spat in her face. Then he came rushing out the door and pulled us all out to the car." Sophia then took a deep breath, and her voice got very small. "We left the other Mama there on the floor."

Paige then interrupted. "Let me tell the rest, Sophia, okay?" Sophia nodded, placing her head down on the counter, and Paige took over the telling of their story.

"Later, after driving around for an hour, Daddy dropped us off at home and told us to check on Mama. We went into the house but couldn't wake her up, so we called 911. The ambulance man said she had to go to the hospital and asked if we had someone to call to take care of us. Being the oldest, I said yes, we would call our grandmother. The driver asked how old I was, and I told her fifteen. She said that was old enough to take care of the younger ones. So, Mama left in the ambulance, and the driver told us to contact our grandmother."

At this point, I wrapped Sophia in my arms and hugged her as my tears fell freely down my face. Wiping my tears, I told Paige, "Go 'head, honey."

"But we didn't call you because Mama always told us never to call you, Grandma," Paige said. "We were hungry, so I made peanut butter and jelly sandwiches for dinner."

Sophia lifted her head from the counter. "Then she bathed us and put us to bed," she said. "We were happy when Daddy came home late that night before we fell asleep and asked where Mama was," Paige added.

"We told him about the hospital, and he got a funny look on his face," William chimed in.

"Then Daddy told us he had to go to work so that he would bring us over to your house, but not to tell you where Mama was at," Paige said.

"Oh no, the time he said Patsy went on a trip with her girlfriends . . ." I shook my head, "and I praised him for being such a good husband and allowing her to have fun and get some rest with her friends."

After hearing the children tell their stories, all I could envision was Bounce beating Patsy like she was a stranger on the street. And for that, he had to pay. Even if Patsy refused to press charges, I would make sure he would answer for what he did to her. As my inner tirade calmed, I realized

Patsy was also hitting Bounce. She was part of the problem. Shaking off any excuse Bounce might use, I knew he knew she was sick. He was supposed to help her—not hit her back.

The thought ricocheted through my head, *but there was a*

reaction for every action.

Coming out of my trance, I asked the children, "Do you know where your daddy is now?"

"When he dropped us off, he said he was going to my other grandma's house," Sophia responded.

Bounce's mother was in a nursing home but owned a house in New Orleans. That meant he got out of town. And I'm confident he took Patsy with him.

Then during a moment of silence, Sophie stopped swinging her legs and used her finger to trace invisible doodles on the kitchen counter and stated, "I hope Mama and Daddy get a divorce."

Stunned, I asked, "How do you know what a divorce is?"

"From the kids at school. One day after they were fighting, I heard Mama tell Daddy she wanted one. She said she'd been thinking about it. She was the other mama then."

"My friend said her parents have been happier since they divorced. She said she gets gifts from both parents for birthdays *and* Christmas. I think I'd enjoy receiving double the gifts," Sophie continued. "Plus, maybe Mama won't be sick as much if she and Daddy get one. The other mama said he stresses her."

Paige popped Sophia's braid. "We wouldn't be a family then, brat."

Sophia batted her sister's hand away from her. "Stop, Paige. You said the same thing. Things were quiet when Mama and Daddy weren't fighting."

Paige stood up. "But Daddy is not the problem. The other mama is the problem. Daddy hits Mama when she hits him. She should keep her hands to herself."

I was devastated to hear this argument. Bounce and Patsy had created an entire mess.

William, the smallest of them all, looked back and forth between his sisters. He then asked me. "I like being a family, but I don't like the fighting. Do you want them to divorce, Grandma?"

"Maybe," I said. I had no other comment to make in the midst of such craziness. My grandkids were not dumb.

Lord, keep my grandchildren. And although Paige clearly blames both, Bounce knows Patsy is sick. I can't continue to carry this burden of seeking revenge for too much longer. Bounce must die. I have to find him.

All the kids continued talking, but my mind was on New Orleans. I had Bounce's mother's address somewhere on a Christmas card I saved. I made a mental note to find it. And as soon as I did, I would make the nine- hour drive from Decatur to New Orleans. The long drive would give me enough time to devise a plan to give Bounce the bullet he deserved. I knew if I found him, I'd find Patsy.

"Hey, guys, did you forget you were watching the movie? One of your favorites, I might add. Let me go and get it started back up for you."

"Thanks, Grandma. It's probably better the second time around, anyway," William said, sliding off the stool.

"Second time?"

Paige and Sophia giggled and high- fived each other. "We already saw it with Aunt Carolyn," William said, skipping out of the room.

It seemed I was always a dollar short behind Ms. Carolyn, and it was beginning to grind me in a *not*-so-special way.

CHAPTER TEN

After setting the movie back to its place. I left the kids and went into my bedroom to shuffle through my desk drawer where I last remembered placing some of my correspondence.

"Aha!" I shouted in victory when I pulled the weathered envelope out of the drawer.

Looking around and making sure Malcolm and MJ were somewhere else in the house. I folded the envelope with the returned address and placed it in my purse.

Next, I had to produce a believable story that would not upset Malcolm about my having to travel alone.

I could hear Malcolm coming down the hall, so I hastily opened my phone. "Yes,girl, I am so sorry, but I'm here for you. I'll do my best to be there as soon as possible."

Malcolm walked in on the tail end of my fake call, just as I had planned. "Go where, Trish?"

"That was Lorraine. She has an emergency and needs me desperately. I told her I would come because maybe helping her would take my mind off Patsy and Bounce. I need to do something. This sitting here is driving me crazy."

Malcolm stood and stared at me. His motionless regard had me ready to confess that it was all a lie and that I was going to kill Bounce. I opened my mouth, but he cut me off.

"Maybe that's just what you need. But didn't you tell MJ you would help him pick out a ring?"

I slapped my hand across my face. "Shoot! I sure did. What do you think I should do, Malcolm? Lorraine has always been there for me. Maybe this should be a father and son event, picking out the ring?"

Rubbing his chin, Malcolm slowly grinned. "I must admit, it would be a good way to bring some sunshine into my day." He then rubbed his palms together. "We can even go out to dinner later. Paige is old enough to watch the kids. I can order pizza for them."

Lord, if I have to repent for murder, I might as well repent for lying too.

After taking a long, hot shower, I promised myself if I felt different when I came out of the bathroom, I wouldn't go. But instead, I felt a sense of empowerment. I was feeling energetic for the first time in days.

Malcolm walked in while I lotioned my body.

"You sure you okay to drive? You haven't had much sleep."

"Oh, I would say that the medicine of being held and loved by you put me to sleep and then gave me the energy to make this drive," I said, unable to look Malcolm fully in the face. I hated lying to my husband.

Lord, I promise I'll do right when this is all over.

I quickly packed an overnight bag and included my family Bible with my weapon and ammunition tucked inside. I put it on the backseat and jumped into the driver's seat with a new vengeance.

After putting Bounce's mother's address in the GPS, I

headed to New Orleans, determined to kill my son-in-law. Consumed with hatred, I sought to rid the earth of this wife beater.

~~~

I've been in New Orleans for two hot, humid, and rainy days. I forgot how miserable the summer weather was this far south. I was staking out Bounce's mother's home. And I didn't know how the police did it. It was the most boring job ever, like watching paint peel. The long wait also meant I was scared I would run out of gas if I used my air conditioner so I sparingly ran it to save on gas, but I was hot as hades in a "Saints Go Marching In" parade. I didn't want to leave to put more gas in the car in case I missed Bounce or Patsy. And by now, my shirt and pants were sticking to my sweaty body.

I'm dressed all wrong. Somebody should have written a manual, "What to Wear to a Stakeout."

I refused to leave to go to Walmart to get appropriate summer clothing to keep cool. I just sat in that car waiting and watching the steam rising like smoke from the asphalt street. If I ended up needing to go to the bathroom, I was going to bust out crying. In my haste, I had failed to plan well. My clothing was an illustration of my thoughtless need for revenge. The old saying is true. Make plans in haste, repent in leisure. And I was repenting. Maybe not the way God would like me to, but I was so sorry I was in this car, in this heat, feeling so foolish.

Talk on the radio of an approaching hurricane brought vivid memories of the horrors of Hurricane Katrina, which caused devastating flooding in New Orleans in August of 2005. I had no intention of witnessing another catastrophe, so I tuned
~~~

my ears to the weather on my car radio. I needed to finish my business and get out of town if the hurricane came ashore. But if I didn't find Bounce before it hit, I prayed the storm would do my job like it did for those 1,392 Katrina fatalities. I hoped it washed him out to sea and he drowned like in my drowning vision. The storm wouldn't need my help to accomplish that feat. Maybe if I just sat here and prayed, God would do the deed for me.

Yes, I could live with that. What I couldn't live with was Patsy suffering the same demise as Bounce due to the hurricane. I had to find her.

While on the stakeout, I'd actually seen Bounce come out of the house repeatedly, but there was no sign of Patsy. I knocked on the door twice, hoping she'd answer while he was away, but she still never came to the door. I couldn't move forward until all players were in their place. I wouldn't risk getting rid of Bounce and losing Patsy.

I had to consider one thing: What if Patsy wasn't with Bounce?

Once I arrived in the city, I rented a car. I realized on my way here that they would recognize my car. I made sure I rented one with heavily tinted windows. Here I sat, feeling like Colombo across from Bounce's mother's house. With too much idle time, I imagined all kinds of crazy scenarios. What if Bounce had hurt Patsy? What if he had her tied up in the basement? What if he had killed her and she was in his freezer?

"Jesus," I prayed, "I want to lay eyes on my child."

I felt hot all over and felt the nudge of the Holy Spirit say, "Why are you calling on Jesus? You have taken charge of this situation. Have you forgotten that all things happen for the good of those who love and follow His commandments?"

My eyes widened, and I trembled. But then I felt my heart harden, "Well, you all are certainly taking your time. How about I give Him help with this one?"

After sitting in the heat for two more hours, I decided to speak to Bounce face-to- face the next time he returned home. Of course, I'd bring my gun with me if I needed it. But, darn, even if I didn't, I might shoot him anyway.

As soon as I saw Bounce pull into the driveway, I started my car, whipped it behind him, and jumped out of it, not bothering to close the door.

He looked as if he'd seen a ghost once he got out of the car and noticed me approaching him. After leaving a hundred death threats on his voicemail, I understood why.

"Where is she?" I kept my hand inside my purse, ready.

"Trish . . ."

"Don't call me by my name!" I yanked my hand from my purse and waved the gun in his face. Bounce slowly backed up the driveway.

"Where is she?" I snarled. "She's not here," he stuttered.

"Where is she?" I barked again, waving my gun in the air.

"I said she's not here!" He was bolder this time, not afraid of me or my gun. Almost annoyed. Staring into his troubled face, Bounce seemed tired. His eyes appeared sunken, and his face was full of scruffy stubble. My eyes swept over his wrinkled shirt and hunched shoulders. He seemed miserable.

"I trusted you with my child, and you put your hands on her." My hands shook with the gun pointed at his chest.

"Trish, put the gun down." "Or what?"

"You don't want to do this," he mumbled.

"Don't tell me what I want to do," I roared.

"You don't understand!"

"*What* don't I understand, huh? I saw what you did to her! I saw the bruises on her face and her broken limbs. You spat on her when she was lying on the kitchen floor. Do you know the children told me that?" My blood was boiling, and I saw red.

"Your grandkids need you, Trish.

Patsy needs you," he said.

"No, she needs a husband who will care for her, not hit her."

"I've taken care of her the best I know how."

"By pounding on her?"

"I'm getting too old for this mess."

Bounce gritted his teeth in frustration. "It's not how it appears."

"It's not how it seems?" I cackled. "Seems like I saw Patsy laid up in the hospital, beaten, bruised, and eyes swollen shut. It's *exactly* how it appears." I placed my finger on the trigger.

"Put the gun down, Trish."

I threw my head back and chuckled. Not because any of this was funny but because I knew I was about to let my craziness prevail.

"We fought. Often. That's what married people do."

"No, they do not, Bounce. My husband has never put his hands on me," I screeched.

"Everyone doesn't have a perfect marriage like yours."

"My marriage is far from perfect," I murmured, thinking of the affair in our marriage and my neglect.

"You put your hands on my child! You had no right to put your blasted hands on her."

Then without thinking, I squeezed the trigger. I didn't mean to do it; really, I didn't. I-I don't understand why. I just did.

Bounce touched all over his chest. "You were going to shoot me!"

I pulled the trigger again—but nothing happened.

Snatching the gun from my hands, Bounce checked the chamber.

"No bullets."

With an unbelievably distorted look on my face, I screamed, "No, you should be dead."

Malcolm had to have taken them out of the chamber. My heart thudded like a wild horse in a corral. I had trouble catching my breath when I realized I was really going to do it. I would have to thank my husband for keeping me from committing murder.

"Get away from here." Bounce threw the gun away. "And stay away from me. You're as crazy as your daughter is." He turned his back and left me standing there, still trying to catch my breath.

Again, my life flashed before my eyes. It started on the day I got married and was followed by the birth of my two kids. Then suddenly, I saw myself sitting in a prison cell. My tireless work for my family was gone in the blink of an eye had I gotten my way.

Thank you, God.

I got into my car, holding my breath until I drove off. The one question I feared most and was never answered pounded against my brain.

Where's Patsy?

CHAPTER ELEVEN

While driving back to Decatur, I finally allowed the Holy Spirit to speak to me again. Before I hit the state of Alabama, the Holy Spirit began our conversation.

I heard Him say in my spirit, "It's time to practice what you taught the ladies in your Bible study group. When down, go where you can find hope. Go to your HOPE, Trish. He's waiting for you."

Tears flowed as my heart softened a bit. Thankfully, I was near a rest stop. I pulled in and allowed the Holy Spirit to minister to me.

"He's still your Father. He's your Jehovah Shalom, the God of Peace. Allow Him to bring the peace you're seeking in your life. Don't let the voice of the dark one continue to reign in your head. His job is to lead you down a path of destruction. Take the blinders of temptation off and open your heart."

Finally, I said, "I hear you, Lord; I'm repenting and getting back into fellowship with you, God." I moaned, asking God for forgiveness, and praying for my return to trust God to answer my prayer and help me find Patsy and bring some peace back into my life. I said this mantra repeatedly until I felt my faith shift.

"Lord, help my unbelief."

I cried cleansing tears this time. With a renewed spirit and feeling lighter with a sense of peace, I dried my eyes and got back on Highway I-85 North. I had a new perspective. God was going to fight my battles for me.

Arriving home tired but at more peace than I had since this ordeal began, I went into my house, passing small children's shoes scattered haphazardly over the hallway floor. I breathed in the scent of recently popped popcorn and saw the evidence of small bowls stacked in the kitchen sink. Cutting off the overhead light Malcolm had left on over the stove, I dragged my suitcase into the bedroom.

Malcolm turned over and reached for my hand. "Everything all right?"

"Uh-huh. Lorraine is where she should be," I said, tired of lying but not wanting to fight over where I had really been. I was exhausted and ready to lay it all down. Climbing out of my clothes and crawling next to Malcolm, I spooned him. He reached back and hugged me to him, and I snuggled into his back. "'Night," I slurred as I instantly fell asleep.

~~~

Sunday morning, the family went to service at our neighborhood church, Standing on the Rock Interdenominational Church, where we had been members since returning to Decatur.

Since I had not been to a service for a while, the Children's Church staff receptionist had turned over and did not recognize me. Since the children and I did not have the same last names, I had to show my custody paperwork when I tried to drop the
~~~

kids off at Sunday school. Security had tightened after an unauthorized person picked up a child without the parents' permission. An Amber Alert was issued and the church had to explain why the child was released to someone not listed on the intake form.

Nothing's simple anymore.

After getting the children settled, we ventured into the sanctuary. Once inside the seemingly standing-room only crowd, we were ushered into two available seats. I thought about my involvement with Standing on the Rock Church and its leader, Pastor Troy. He was handsome, with a bodybuilder's physique. Like Barry White, his voice always drew a crowd, and his pecan-tan skin, brown eyes, and compassionate nature kept them.

The people exalted him in Decatur and he held leadership positions in the community. He based his sermons on scripture and gave us current life applications to follow in today's society. He was a sought- after speaker with his evenings and weekends filled. I was excited to be in his presence and hear what he had for me that day.

As the choir continued to sing, I realized how much I missed singing with them. I began to think that I might join again someday soon.

I'd stopped singing during one of Patsy's episodes two or three years before. During that season, I had custody of the grandkids for about two months and couldn't attend practice. It's where I first got custody papers of the kids that we never changed. The number of times we had the kids, it was important we had something in writing to give us authority in cases of accidents. When the kids returned to their parents' home, I had adjusted to skipping rehearsal twice a week and just never returned to a commitment I had previously loved. But how could I expect Him to serve me if I didn't serve Him? Although I quit the choir, I continued serving God by conducting a weekly Bible study group in my home.

A year ago, after my involvement in Pastor Troy's class on spiritual gifts, he appointed me to lead the Women's Bible study group. He saw more in me than I saw in myself. He was good at identifying spiritual gifts and helping others understand their calling.

During Bible study, I followed Pastor Troy's example by helping the group's members identify their spiritual gifts and walking in their purpose. Although spiritual gift assessment helped identify service in the church, I assisted them in identifying income streams based on their spiritual gifts. Finally, I told them that God specifically placed them on earth, which meant He gave them the provision to provide for their livelihood. As a result, half of the ladies became entrepreneurs.

Standing with my hands lifted in praise and worship, I enjoyed the choir, but I thought the choir sang a little longer than usual. I needed a word and was ready for the preaching to begin. Although the Holy Spirit and I regularly communed, I needed to hear Pastor Troy's encouragement to ease my troubled heart and weary mind.

While waiting for the sermon to start, my mind wandered. I scanned the congregation as Malcolm clapped to the beat of the drums. I noticed Carolyn wasn't sitting in her usual spot. Part of me wanted to see her. However, no matter what was happening in her life, Carolyn never missed church. Not even fooling around with random men kept her away.

About that time, I heard Pastor Troy say, "The devil comes to steal, kill, and destroy. Don't let him have his way." The sermon resonated in my spirit, and I went to the altar for prayer during the altar call.

Standing at the altar, I lifted my hands and asked God to deliver me from my madness. "You're going to make it. This is only a test," Pastor Troy said. "And you *will* pass this test."

I prayed, "Please send her back home, God—healed." Not that He'd listen to a woman who just tried to commit murder.

The pastor prayed for me; however, I struggled to receive it. But my desire to kill Bounce diminished. Sadly, the feeling didn't last long.

I'm more than a feeling, daughter.

Pressing forward, I asked God to restore my mind and heart.

When I left the altar, I was in a daze. It was because the night before, as tired as I was, I wasn't sleeping well and had nightmares about Patsy.

As we gave our tithes and offerings, Carolyn stood and walked to the baskets to give her contribution. I did a double take when the woman who walked behind her was the very woman who had slept with Malcolm. Carolyn turned and said something to her, and she smiled as they went and sat down together.

I glared at them as they took seats next to each other. Carolyn refused to look in my direction, but the other woman did. Her smirk was almost my undoing.

What the heck is Carolyn trying to pull?

I was livid. I turned to Malcolm and whispered, "I feel ill," grabbing his arm. I yanked him and we left that minute.

Unaware of the drama unfolding, Malcolm got the kids from the children's church while I went straight to the car.

Leaning against the car and hyperventilating, I closed my

eyes. I could envision the sanctuary and knew that nothing but the grace of God stopped me from leaping across those pews, snatching Carolyn by her hair, and slinging her into the pulpit. I instantly lost all respect for her. The enemy of my enemy is my friend.

This messiness must've been Carolyn's new truth. All I'm going to say is that God doesn't enjoy ugly. And if she's befriending the one woman who contributed to the worst days of my life to get my attention, she's making the wrong move. She's playing with a madwoman.

Following the service, the ride home from church was silent. The grandbabies were asleep or with headphones on their ears in the backseat and Malcolm stared straight ahead without speaking to me. I didn't want to talk to him anyway because I was in a mood.

Later that afternoon, after we got home and had dinner, I began thinking about Carolyn and her escapade that Sunday morning during church. Her sitting with the woman from Malcolm's affair made me relive Malcolm's infidelity and I was furious with him again. I called Carolyn to give her a piece of my mind, but she didn't answer my call. Knowing Malcolm and I would be there, I wanted to know what possessed her to bring Malcolm's ex-mistress to church with her. Was she trying to start a war?

The woman with whom Malcolm had an affair was named Dianna. She's only in her thirties and she's gorgeous. Malcolm, in guilt, confessed. The night he told me, I forced him to show me a picture of her. It devastated me because I understood why and how she would attract any man. She's Black and Asian mixed with that exotic touch men seem to drool over. And here she comes sashaying into my church with my ex-best friend, long, black hair flowing, and built like the Commodores' "Brick House" song was playing with her every step. It was such a lonely time in my marriage. I made Malcolm divulge what he knew about her. I'm not sure why we do that—we want to hear every detail—knowing it only brings us more pain.

He wouldn't divulge everything but he confessed why he slept with her. He said, "Trish, it was because she listened to me, even when I wasn't talking."

Angry and confused, I screamed, "Whatever does that mean?"

Malcolm sighed as though it pained him to explain it to me. "She's in tune with my needs without me having to tell her."

He continued to give me the details that nailed the coffin to my self-esteem for months afterward. Details like she was single, never married, and had no kids. She knew he had a wife because he'd told her, but she told him that he was a good man and deserved more than he was getting at home. In the end, she just didn't care.

Other than pictures, I've never met her. But her image was branded in my brain. I didn't know where she worked or lived; Malcolm wouldn't tell me those pieces of information, and trust me, I'd tried to get it out of him because I wanted to beat respect and morals into her.

I wanted to face the woman who had taken my husband from me, if even for a night or two. But I never got the chance.

After a while, I was done with wanting to face her, confront her, or whoop up on her. It no longer mattered. I had my husband and my marriage, which were all that mattered.

Never in a million years had I planned to tell Carolyn's secret, but if you make a person mad enough, there's no telling what they might do. And Carolyn is making me see red. Drive a hammer in my skull mad. Right now, I can't remember the good times we once had. But I had to be better than this hurt, and my love for her outweighed my anger, so I knew I would continue to keep her secret.

CHAPTER TWELVE

It'd been a week since I searched for Patsy in New Orleans, and I still hadn't heard from her. Then, of course, punk Bounce called to tell my husband I tried to shoot him. Malcolm was so angry he refused to speak to me.

Luckily, he knew me well enough to remove the bullets from the gun before I got my hands on it. But that also meant he realized *I* was wrapped in crazy.

Most days, I wondered if I was coming or going. I was all over the place at work. My grandbabies kept me busier than ever, and even though MJ had left again, he wanted help planning the proposal. Yet, no matter how overwhelmed I became, nothing kept me from worrying about Patsy.

On our way home from church the following Sunday, Malcolm called my name. "Trish?"

The sound of his voice caused me to roll my eyes. He was going to once again talk about allowing the Lord to take care of the situation with Bounce. And I was over it. But to my surprise, he announced, "I know where Patsy is."

My heart dropped. "What?"

"She called me yesterday." Seeing my shock, he rushed to explain. "She made me promise not to tell you where she is, but she told me to tell you she's better and working on herself."

"She called you and you didn't *tell* me?" I tried my best not to slap him silly. "She made me promise," he sighed.

"She didn't want to talk to you." "Why?"

"Because she feels like she disappointed you."

"Where is she?" My hands shook in disbelief. "How have *I* become the problem?" I sighed.

"I can't tell you where she is, but she's nearby. She's in therapy, trying to get herself together." He glanced at me. "She's filing for a divorce from Bounce."

"She'd better."

Malcolm didn't respond.

"Please tell me where she is. I want to look at her and see her for myself. That's the only thing that will give me any peace." I was close to begging.

"She's well, Trish. This is a journey that she has to take alone. You can't save her. Only God can save her."

"When is she coming home?"

"All she told me was she was coming back soon. Give her time, Trish."

Malcolm stopped at the red light and turned to me. "Patsy will mail the kids' information for their birth certificates and medical cards, and she said we could sign up for benefits when we get them."

"We don't need help to feed the kids. We're fine." I turned toward the window and glued my eyes to the car next to us. The brat in the backseat stuck her tongue out at me. Just not my day. I sighed and turned back to my husband. "If Patsy's doing all that, that must mean she doesn't plan to return to Bounce, which is a good thing. But I also get the feeling that she's not coming back to get these babies for a while, either."

"She's doing the best she can, Trish.

And she isn't far."

The wheels inside my head spun. *If she is close, where is she?*

I calculated Patsy's life in my head. Patsy only had two friends, Carolyn, whom I used to speak to daily, and her childhood friend. The last time I checked with either, they said they hadn't heard from her and were just as worried as I was about her. At least, that's what they told me. The last time I tried calling Carolyn after she pulled that stunt in church, she didn't pick up.

I took a long breath; my mind was racing. I should have taken comfort in Malcolm knowing where Patsy was and that she was safe. But that wasn't enough for me. I needed to know where she was and that she was well. The watered-down version she gave her father wouldn't suffice—I wanted the truth for myself.

While pondering Patsy's whereabouts, my cell phone vibrated. It was Daddy. I hadn't talked to him since our argument about Bounce beating Patsy. So, I ignored his call, sending him to voicemail.

"You need to talk to your father," Malcolm said.

"Nope." I stared out the window.

Honestly, it shouldn't have surprised me once I thought about it. Daddy was very overprotective of my sister and me. He allowed us to date when we were sixteen, and even then, we had to double date. I remember when our male friends left our home walking because our curfew was so early, and their rides hadn't come for them.

Daddy treated us like princesses, but he hit my mother, mostly when she came home drunk and started fights with him. Now when I think about it, he was physically abusive at times.

I never put the hitting and shoving in that context before. *Now I get it.* Daddy understands Bounce's behavior because he experienced similar issues with my mother. Mom passed away from an aneurysm seven years ago. And with all the reevaluating I'm doing to see things through a more objective eye, I have to wonder if that was due to their altercations.

Daddy ensured my brothers understood that putting their hands on a woman was wrong but justified Bounce's actions. Thinking about it now and how Mama used to come at him, leaving him no choice but to defend himself, I could see why he felt like he did about Patsy putting her hands on Bounce. But Patsy was nothing like my mother. Not to mention she had a reason. She was mentally ill. My mother's only excuse was going ten drinks past her limit before coming home to take her anger out on the people she was supposed to love the most.

But was her drinking masking a mental disorder?

As I sat in the car, my mind ran in circles, wondering which it was, alcohol that chased demons or demons that imbibed on alcohol? It was the chicken or egg effect.

My cell phone vibrated again, and I grumbled.

"You can't ignore him forever," Malcolm grunted.

My eyes slowly slid closed. "Watch me."

Once, after having a stupid argument with my mother over the phone, I'd gone five years without talking to her, which was easy to do. She was a monster. And I could be the princess of petty.

The day I finally answered her call, Mama said, "May I speak to Patsy?" Meet the queen of petty.

Mama spent the entire conversation talking about me to my child. Then finally, Patsy asked me, "Mama, did you do those things Grandmother said?"

"Of course not," I exclaimed. It was difficult to explain that my mother was a drunkard and blamed me for her misfortunes because I reminded her of my father.

Finally, I had enough of my mother's nonsense and completely cut her out of my life. We were living overseas, and I declined all her calls, utterly unbothered by not reaching out to her on birthdays or holidays. I did what was best for me. As a child, I had no choice but to deal with my mother.

Those five years of not speaking to her were my most peaceful, drama-free years. When I finally talked to her again, she apologized, but I didn't believe her. Mama had done too much to be sorry. She didn't even remember half of what she'd done to me. I wished I could've let it all go before she left this earth, but I couldn't.

Forgiveness is so darn hard. I would talk to Daddy when I was ready. I was curious myself to know when that day would come . . . if ever.

CHAPTER THIRTEEN

I worked part-time for a company that did medical billing coding. Instead of offices, we worked in small cubicles with desks, chairs, and phones. Being claustrophobic, I spent more time outside my cubicle than sitting in it. However, at least I managed to meet my weekly data input quota. Lynette, my work friend, often helped if I came up short.

The Monday after being off for a week due to Patsy's absence and my grandkids' presence, I returned to work. After clocking in, I heard, "You're late again, Trish," my boss Geraldine growled.

I didn't want to be bothered. "I know, but my grandbabies weren't cooperating this morning."

"I don't care," she shrugged. "If you're late again, I will have to let you go."

"I'm doing the best I can, Geraldine." Trying to keep from crying, I wiped my hands down my face. "Please bear with me until my daughter comes home. I promise I will make up any time I need."

"All right, Trish. I'm not insensitive to your circumstances. But I have a business to run. Please let me know when you'll be late, so I can make sure someone covers for you."

"Thank you so much for understanding, Geraldine. I won't let you down," I said with a sigh of relief.

The entire six years I'd been at the agency, I couldn't stand Geraldine. And if Patsy's children weren't staying with me, I would've walked back out when she started in on me.

The problem wasn't that Malcolm didn't earn enough money to support us. I just needed my own money for extras around the house. We'd paid off our mortgage, and Malcolm handled all the household bills. Anything I earned went toward shopping, vacations, and date nights. Right now, anything extra we had was for our grandbabies.

Malcolm retired from the military years ago when we settled here in Decatur. Even though he received his retirement pay, he was bored with nothing to do. So, he got a job with the State as a GS-12, which pays a salary in six figures. We had problems at this point in our lives, but money wasn't one of them. "Is Patsy still missing?" Lynette asked.

"Malcom knows where she is, so I wouldn't say missing. But she still hasn't come home yet."

Lynette placed her hand on her ample hip. "Huh? Why didn't she tell you?"

"I'm not sure," I complained. "It could be because of how I've acted throughout all this and that I pulled out a gun on her husband."

"You *what*?" Lynette said. She then sat and swiveled her seat to face mine.

"I sure did. And I squeezed the trigger too," I beamed. "Unfortunately, Malcolm had removed the bullets from the gun."

Wondering if I should have kept my mouth shut, I continued, "In the meantime, Patsy's distancing herself as far away from me as possible."

"Aw, Shug, I've been praying God keeps her safe and protects her and comforts you," Lynette said, trying to console me.

"From your lips to His ears," I nodded. "I'm in a constant state of praying and then arguing with God. It's not a pretty sight. Even I realize that I'm coming unglued."

"I can't imagine what you're going through," Lynette said, her eyes shining with tears for me.

"My daughter needs to come home. I want her to get a divorce. She and the kids can move in with us for a while if she wants to. I just want her to get her life back on track, take her meds, and live her best."

"I'm sure Patsy knows she has a home to return to whenever she's ready." Lynette's hands waved as she spoke. I noticed her ring finger was bare. She always wore a beautiful three-carat diamond wedding ring that the ladies on the job often admired.

"Where's your wedding ring?" Lynette and I celebrated our twenty-fifth wedding anniversary this year, and never once had I seen her without her ring. It was the same with me. I'd only removed my ring once in thirty years because Malcolm upgraded it for a new one. Even when he cheated on me, that ring stayed on my finger. It was the one thing that reminded me I was the woman Malcolm chose—the woman he loved.

"With all you're going through, I didn't want to worry you with my problems, Trish. I'm getting divorced."

Now it was my mouth that gapped open with disbelief. But I composed myself enough to say, "No way! Stop playing, girl. Is it being cleaned? I know you're joking with me. This is *not* the way to try to get me to laugh." When Lynette's facial expression didn't change or break out with a "gotcha," I became concerned.

"We don't believe in divorce, Lynette. Right? We always said we'd never divorce our husbands, no matter what, that our marriages were built on godly principles," I said, looking her in the eyes.

Lynette nodded. "Jacob and I tried recommendations designed to keep marriages together. We spent time and money on marriage counseling. Our pastor counseled us and had us praying together every morning and evening. We even tried couples' Bible study. Nothing helped. We just aren't happy anymore."

"What does happiness have to do with it? Have you lost your joy in the Lord?" I rolled my chair closer to hers. "Have you allowed Satan to fool you into thinking there is something better outside of marriage?"

Lynette gave me that look that said, do you hear what *you're* saying?

Knowing I was a hypocrite with how I acted, I asked myself if my behavior ruined my testimony like Malcolm told me it would.

Lynette seemed to struggle to believe it herself. "I still love my husband, and I know he loves me. But we're just not *in* love with each other."

Lynette folded her arms across her chest. "Honestly, I haven't been in love with him for years. But the older I get, the more I realize what love is and what it means to me." "What do you mean you are just realizing what love is?" I quickly interjected.

Lynette stood as if she did not hear me and emphatically said, "You know what I mean. He's just not it. I've tried my hardest to make it work."

"No, I don't know," I said, trying to get a real concrete

answer.

I stood and started to pace between her and my small cubicle as she continued her confession. "I've done what I thought I was supposed to do. But now, I'm ready for a change. I'm only fifty years old. Whatever time I have left on this earth, I want to spend it with a smile on my face."

Hitting her right fist in her left hand as I continued to pace, Lynette said convincingly, "I want to be happy, and my husband hasn't made me happy for an exceptionally long time. We both were good at pretending over the years. I don't want to pretend anymore."

I was stunned. "Wow. I'm sorry to hear this, but I understand you feel you must do what's best for you." I considered the ramifications of them splitting up for a moment. "Since he's a deacon, what will he tell the church?

"You know the church administrators are firm believers that divorce shouldn't be an option unless adultery is involved. Not even then if both parties are believers and understand forgiveness. Adultery isn't the issue . . . right?" I asked with caution.

Staring at me with a questioning look, Lynette answered, "No! At least, I don't think so. And I don't care what my soon-to-be ex-husband tells the church. I'm tired of the people at that church. I don't want to be a deacon's wife anymore."

"Umm, you seemed happy with your role as deacon's wife."

"The obligations and responsibilities are over for me. I've had enough church to last me the rest of my life. I'm never going back. Don't get me wrong. I'm not leaving my relationship with God. I'll take God with me wherever the wind may carry me, but what the church folks think about my decision isn't my problem or concern. I want to be free."

"Free? What does it mean to be free?" I inquired.

"You are free to do what you please. Free to go wherever you want to go whenever you want. Now that I think about it, I've never been free," Lynette said. "I want to be free from the gossip about my clothes or how my hair looks."

"When did you hear members discussing your clothes?"

Lynette didn't answer me. She was so caught up in complaining about the life she felt forced to live and the scrutiny she lived under.

"I'm tired of the first lady and church mothers telling me how a deacon's wife should act and present herself publicly. They suggested I take an etiquette and speech class after asking me to present at one of the big statewide church conferences." She then huffed but continued her complaints.

"When I sought counsel from the pastor, his wife had the nerve to insinuate that I wanted to have an affair with *her* husband because I didn't want her in the room to discuss her and the church mothers. The woman had the nerve to tell me she doesn't allow him to meet with females without her presence. So, I didn't set the appointment. After speaking to Pastor in the receiving line after service, he did."

She continued with tears revealing the pain she felt inside. "I could have put up with that, but my husband, the so-called deacon, never stood up for me and did nothing to protect me. He acted as if he agreed with them. He never confronted them on my behalf. So I want to be free from the hurt that church caused me."

I sympathized as best as I could by giving her a gentle hug. I knew we were at work, and I was hoping others had on their headphones as they worked because Lynette was spilling a lot of her concerns over the office airwaves. But I had done the same, and sometimes, you just had to get it out. I wouldn't be a friend if she listened to my problems, and I didn't reciprocate.

"You know, you're making me think about what freedom looks like. I went straight from my parent's house to a husband, then came the responsibilities of being a mother, and now taking care of my grandbabies. Maybe I don't know how freedom truly looks or feels. But we both need to look at freedom from a godly perspective."

Slumping down in her chair, Lynette spun her chair back to her computer and began typing medical codes into the system.

"Well, it has nagged me all my day hours and haunted me in my sleep. And at this point, I'm not changing my mind. I'm going through with this divorce. I've already found a place to live."

I had also turned back to my computer screen, but I spun around and tapped Lynette on the shoulder when she said that. "Wait, you're giving up your house? You love that house."

"No, I don't. I was playing a role, making our house a home, but I've always wanted to live in the city. I don't want any part of that house—or him—anymore. The condominium I found is nice. Over the next four months, I have three trips booked, and I am leaving this job. I want to see the world, and I will do that. I'm taking my savings and will live how I've always wanted."

I squeaked, then lowered my voice. "You're *quitting*? My goodness, how much do you have saved?" I was now curious.

"Twenty years' worth of pinching pennies. I rarely ever touched any of my earned income. Robert paid for everything. He didn't allow me to carry any of our household expenses, and over the years, I dabbled in investing. If I budget right, I have enough money to live comfortably for a long while. At least until I can apply for Social Security and my pension from here."

I nervously chuckled. "I think I'm jealous." However, there was seriousness behind my laughter.

"Don't be jealous! You have a wonderful life with a great husband who loves you. Think of your kids and grandkids. You've traveled the world and have a home that you love. Your life is full."

I grunted as though she was wrong, but inside, I knew God had blessed me. "If you say so," I sighed. "Where are you going first?"

I listened to Lynette talk about her upcoming trip to Greece as she continued to work. Then, a little later, I settled into my seat, kicked out my work, and daydreamed about good things until I quit for the day. When the clock showed five, I walked out of the building.

After leaving work, I sat in my car at a red light. I tapped my finger against the steering wheel while listening to the oldies on the radio. Then when I glanced across the street, I couldn't believe my eyes.

"What in the . . ." I almost cursed. Bounce was across the street, opening the door for Carolyn as she hopped into her car. Then he lingered behind, waiting for her to drive away.

Startled when the person in the car behind me blared its horn, I hit the gas and dug for my cell phone in my purse. After finding it, I called Carolyn's phone.

"Hello?" All I heard was static and wind.

"Why were you with Bounce?" I shouted.

"Hello?" Carolyn repeated.

"Girl, you know you can hear me. Why were you with

Bounce?"

"How do you know that?" she stammered.

"I. Saw. You."

All I could hear was Carolyn breathing heavily.

"Carolyn?"

"What?" she screamed.

"Don't you scream at me. I asked you a question."

"Where are you?" she asked, calmer. I pulled the phone away from my mouth. "Why. Were. You. With. Bounce?"

"Chill, Trish," Carolyn coaxed. "He asked me out to lunch."

"Why would he ask you out to lunch?"

"He wanted to talk." "Talk about what?"

My heart was racing. "About you, Patsy. The situation."

"What about it?"

"He said things got out of control."

"The only thing out of control is his hands! What concern is any of this of yours? Of all people, why would Bounce want to discuss these things with you?"

Carolyn didn't respond. "Carolyn, what is going on?" "Trish—"

"*What* is going on?" I yelled again at her. "Don't you play with me."

"I just want you to know that it wasn't intentional."

"What wasn't intentional, Carolyn?"

She took a deep breath before answering. "The affair."

CHAPTER FOURTEEN

The following weekend, MJ came for a visit from his duty station at Fort Bragg, NC. He brought the beautiful woman of his dreams with him, Clara. I could tell by the look in her eyes she loved MJ as much as he loved her. It was refreshing to my soul to see my son happy.

It was a relief knowing Clara understood military life. She wouldn't resent it like I did the more I became part of it. Being an army wife was scary; I was too young and unprepared for the job. Still, I handled it better than most and made the best of it.

Our backyard was perfect for MJ's proposal, and we had arranged a small dinner party with our family and friends. Carolyn was not invited, and Patsy was still absent, but I didn't want to think about that when there was so much love and happiness in the room.

Malcolm and I sat getting to know Clara, stalling until MJ popped the question. Beautiful flowers decorated the gazebo, and the most exquisite wine was breathing in an ice bucket, ready for the toast when she said yes.

As we had rehearsed, I dropped my handkerchief on the ground, and MJ scrambled to pick it up for me. But instead of retrieving it, he dropped to one knee and pulled a Tiffany's teal jewelry box from under the table. When he opened it, flashed the ring to Clara, and asked her to be his wife, I almost screamed, "Yes!" for her. Through tears, she agreed to be his wife. MJ didn't hesitate to place the ring on her finger.

"Whoooooooo!" the guests yelled in unison, erupting in applause.

Malcolm popped the cork and poured the wine into the glasses on the table before him. Picking up mine, I stood and gave my toast.

"I pray that love and happiness fill this marriage," I began the blessing.

"I pray you work together as a team and stick it out when things get tough. Trust me; they *will* get tough." I briefly glanced at Malcolm, then back to MJ and Clara. "I pray you have beautiful children and that you will enjoy life together."

Sitting down, I finished the rest of my thoughts in private. *And I pray you remain honest and faithful because affairs can send you straight to the pits of hell!*

I nodded when appropriate and gave half smiles as the celebration continued around me, but as much as I fought it, my mind was elsewhere.

My best friend had an affair with my son-in-law. I wished my arms were long enough to reach and pull the knife out of my back to stop the pain.

Lost in the memory of Carolyn's confession, I traveled where I said I wouldn't go today. I walked back down memory lane.

"I had an affair with Bounce," Carolyn confessed, the wind howling in the background as we both drove our cars in separate directions.

"You've been sleeping with my daughter's husband?" I barked. "Talk about a fast curveball. I didn't see this coming.

How could you do this?"

Carolyn exhaled. "The affair was brief. We never meant it to happen. I tried cutting it off, but Bounce sucked me back in every time. I'm so sorry. Patsy found out about us, which sparked their last fight."

Losing control, I screamed, "If that's the case, what happened to Patsy is both your fault. You are her godmother and know what she's going through mentally, emotionally, and physically. How could you jeopardize her life for sex?" I put her in the same category as Bounce. "You're on my hit list," I warned.

How do I navigate this kind of betrayal?

"Mom? Are you still with us?" MJ tapped my arm, bringing me out of my musing.

"Absolutely!" I flashed a bright smile. I hugged my son and his future wife. "The two of you make a beautiful couple. I'm so proud of you."

I sent them off with a kiss before they greeted other family members, some of whom had waited in the house to congratulate them. Then with everyone preoccupied, my mind shifted back to Carolyn. She'd never been the type to sleep with someone else's husband, especially since she killed her husband for doing the same.

Carolyn came home from work early one day. After putting a kettle of water on the stove to boil for tea, she went to her bedroom to change into leisure clothes. The bedroom door was closed. Thinking that was odd, she slowly went to turn the doorknob.

But feeling apprehensive that the bedroom door was

closed, she quietly tiptoed to the linen closet first, where she stored her gun and ammunition. Her husband had never wanted her to keep a gun in the house, and the linen closet was the one closet he never touched. They kept a baseball bat by the bed to appease her sense of safety. Loading her gun, she crept back to the bedroom. Inhaling, she placed her hand on the doorknob. Slowly, she opened the bedroom door. . . and to her utter amazement, she found her husband having sex with their neighbor's husband in her bed.

Carolyn said, "Her first reaction was to kill them." So, she immediately lifted her gun and dared them to move. Jumping up together in shock, the men didn't know what to do. They just stood there. Naked. Carolyn resigned herself to the sight of both of them bare to the world after defiling her house and her bed. She couldn't see through her blinding tears and her burning heart.

Since her bedroom was off her kitchen—a design flaw she had always hated—she held the gun on them while deciding what to do next. The promise to throw boiling water on her husband if she ever caught him in her bed with someone else came to mind. So, while still holding the gun on them, Carolyn raced and got the pot of boiling water she put on for tea when she arrived home.

Back in the bedroom, the naked men stood with their hands raised. With the gun in one hand and the pot of hot water in the other, she threw the pot along with the water at her husband. Carolyn said the neighbor started screaming like a girl when her husband fell to the floor. Seeing he was distracted, she grabbed the baseball bat and started whacking the man with it. Then, distraught as they both rolled in agony on the floor, she dared them to get up. Leaving them in the bedroom, Carolyn screamed at them, promised to set fire to the house, and shoot them if they tried to exit it.

Feeling like she had nowhere else to go, Carolyn stumbled out of the house, heaving up her morning's breakfast as she ran to her car. Somehow, she drove to my house. We cried together the entire day until the next night. Malcolm was out of town on a golfing trip with friends, and I was able to be there for my friend. Her pain was my pain.

Carolyn pulled herself together and went home. She returned with a vengeance in her heart. Nothing I said or tried convinced her that she should forgive them. His betrayal was so severe that she woke up in night sweats. The fact that he wouldn't leave the house and continued to expect her to cook and clean for him made Carolyn turn cold. She wanted to kill him.

So, she decided she would. Carolyn did as her husband told her and didn't expose him and his lover. The day she returned home, her husband acted as though what he did was not a problem and that if she had been a better wife and lover, he wouldn't have had to go somewhere else for his satisfaction. He then grabbed her by the neck and told her he had to go to the doctor and get burn medicine for his skin from the damage she had caused. He lied and told the doctor he had dropped a pot of boiling tea on himself. The doctor assured him that the burns were not third-degree and he would recover. He calmly let Carolyn know that was the only reason she wasn't dead or in jail. He then said with cold-blooded intent that the affair would continue until he was ready to stop it.

The next day, Carolyn gave him the first dose of poison in his dinner. She was methodical, determined, and deadly. She poisoned him for over three months. He worked at a chemical plant. She would visit him at work and steal hazardous chemicals. Then she would add drops of them to his food or drink at home.

Her husband began getting sick a few months later. The hospital would blame it on his exposure to the chemicals at his job and advise him to be careful. One night, after going to the hospital with chest pains, he never returned home. He had a heart attack. And it was all because of Carolyn.

She killed her husband, and I was the only person in the world she ever told.

Her husband had been dead for over two years. We were working in her garden at her house, and she reflected on a memory she and her husband had while gardening before he died. Carolyn hunched her shoulders and sobbed. I assumed she was crying because she missed her husband.

I held her in my arms. But it wasn't until she'd wept for about ten minutes that I realized what she was crying about was much bigger. She cried like I cried when I did something wrong that I couldn't bring myself to talk about. So, I questioned her. It didn't take her long to give in and confess. She needed to tell someone and I was there when she unburdened her soul.

The look on her face while telling me what she'd done assured me she had acted out of hurt and a broken heart. She'd killed her husband out of disappointment, embarrassment, and anger.

That day, I emphasized the safety of her secret with me, and I'd meant it. I never planned to tell anyone about what she'd done. She was my best friend. I was the person she could count on for anything . . . and I had believed that I could always count on her.

Why would Carolyn do this to Patsy and our friendship? She had the nerve to ruin my daughter's marriage, knowing I had the power to destroy her life with my knowledge. Was Bounce worth it?

Carolyn told me that Bounce called her and asked about his kids and me. She said he told her he misses them but that they are better off with Malcolm and me. He also told her he had been looking for Patsy and hadn't found her. She also admitted Bounce still loves Patsy and wants her to come home so they can figure things out.

"Over my dead body!" I didn't want Bounce or Carolyn anywhere near my daughter ever again.

According to Carolyn, she and Bounce hadn't had sex in over three months. They stopped a month before the incident with Patsy. Patsy had found out somehow anyway.

Carolyn and Bounce can both kiss me where the sun don't shine, I thought. My friendship with Carolyn was over. She hurt my child. I wanted to return the pain she caused Patsy.

I had to dig deep to control my emotions and not go to Carolyn's house or her job to see if I still had it, as I did back in the day. It would serve her right, whooping her tail up and down the street for her scandalous, backstabbing behavior. One word from me, and she would do time for murder. Shoot, if I never saw Carolyn again, it would be too soon.

Hearing someone laugh brought me back to the celebration at my home, a celebration I was missing because I was stuck on a betrayal my heart didn't want to accept. I needed to move forward. And she needed to stop calling me nonstop daily to gauge my anger. We still hadn't discussed the fact that she brought Malcolm's ex-floozy to our church. Carolyn should be glad I hadn't yet burned down her world.

Turning my head from the guests, I wiped one tear from my eye. I didn't want to shed any tears over Carolyn. One tear was too many. I just hoped her conscience ate her alive and made her tell on herself. It continued to be a hard secret not to tell, but I was a woman of my word and wouldn't expose her, even though she broke our friendship.

MJ made his way back to me.

"Thanks for pulling this together for me so soon, Mama." His genuine smile warmed my heart.

"It was my pleasure, son. I can't wait for the wedding," I chuckled. "Prayerfully, it'll be sooner than later. I'm ready for you two to get married and give me a grandbaby." "You're unable to handle the ones you have now, Ma," he snorted.

Speaking of grandchildren, I headed into the house to check on the kids. They were quiet, which was never a good sign. Silence usually meant trouble where those three were concerned.

I was enjoying my grandbabies. They wore me like an old housecoat, but I wouldn't trade it for anything in this world. They kept me going and full of hope. My mind was more relaxed when I was with them. When I stuck my head into the den, I watched the kids play and eat.

"Sophia, don't boss your brother. Be nice and share," I instructed, then headed to the bathroom.

While I sat on the toilet, my bathroom door flew open. "Carolyn?" She closed the bathroom door behind her. Fear entered my body. I was helpless, so I continued to release my bladder. "What are you doing in my bathroom? Get out!"

Carolyn looked deranged with her tangled tresses and beads of sweat across her upper lip. "I came to talk to you, Trish. You won't take my phone calls. This is the only place I have your unobstructed attention. Please listen to what I have to say."

"That should tell you I don't want to talk to you. Now, get out of my bathroom and out of my house."

Carolyn had seen my goodies throughout our fifteen-year friendship. So, I didn't hesitate to wipe in front of her.

"I never meant to sleep with Bounce. It was a mistake that should never have happened." She frowned. "I was lonely, and he kept making passes at me. It happens. I'm sorry, Trish."

I flushed the toilet.

"Well, it did happen. And my daughter got her tail whooped because of it, then abandoned her kids. Patsy's gone, and I can't find her because of you. *You* are the reason she is missing."

"She's not missing. Patsy doesn't want us to find her."

"Same thing." I washed my hands.

"I don't want to be with Bounce. You realize that, right? What happened between us wasn't love; it was a mistake. Just sex. If I could take it back, I would."

"Could've fooled me. When I saw you with him, you had the biggest smile on your face. You liked being his mistress!"

I brushed past Carolyn and left the bathroom, but she rushed behind me. "Trish, you're my best friend, and I don't want to lose you. I don't *want* Bounce. I'm not sleeping with him. The affair happened and it's over. It will never happen again. It all happened so fast, but I never intended it to happen. I didn't mean for it to. But it did. You realize how out of sorts I've been lately. I've been a little lonely. And it just happened."

"Look, what you and Bounce do is your business," I whispered. "Patsy is divorcing him."

I wanted to step back into the backyard where the proposal

party was taking place, but Carolyn looked a mess, and I didn't want to do anything to hurt MJ and Clara's proposal party.

"Bounce is a loose cannon. You've retaliated before when a man in your life hurt you. Maybe you should choose better. Bounce is a time bomb ready to explode. It's just a matter of time before you're collateral damage. We both know what you're capable of when you're angry. Scratch that. I hope he hurts you to your core. He may end up dead too fooling with you."

Carolyn gasped, looking around to make sure no one overheard me.

"I'm sorry, Trish. You have so much. You don't know how it feels to have nothing and to be lonely in your nothingness. Malcolm treats you like a queen. And Patsy is the only thorn in your rosebush, where I have nothing but weeds."

I snorted in disgust. "You have what you sowed. Look what you're sowing now. You even brought Malcolm's ex-side piece to the church. How could you do that, Carolyn? *Who* are you?"

"I'm your friend who is tired of basking in your shadow. You actually yelled at me because I was a friend of your daughter. She shared her problems with Bounce with *me*. I knew about her struggles because she came to *me!*" she whispered harshly.

"And look how you betrayed her. Look how you betrayed me. I didn't cause your problems. Contrary to your opinion, my life has had enough thorns to last anyone a lifetime. But the good Lord Jesus showed me how to make compost with them. And the thorns made the soil rich, so when I sowed, I harvested mightily."

I then stepped forward, one inch from Carolyn's face.

"Don't you *dare* blame me for your actions. And don't you push me past the grace that is operating in your life right now!"

Once satisfied that I'd dug the knife deep enough, I turned my back on her, stepped outside into the backyard, and sauntered over to mingle with our guests. Ten minutes later, I checked to see if Carolyn was still stalking me and realized she was gone.

"Trish?" The voice didn't surprise me. My daddy had shown up to celebrate MJ's engagement. "Sweetie, I've been calling you."

"Really? Malcolm beats me so much I don't have the time or energy to answer my phone." The sarcasm dripped through my snappy response.

"Stop it, Trish. You know what I mean. You understand how Patsy can get when she's off her meds or in one of her moods. That's all I was saying. I didn't say Bounce was right for putting his hands on my granddaughter, but sometimes—"

"There should never be a *sometimes*! Enjoy the party, Daddy." I kissed his cheek and walked away, trying to muster the strength to celebrate one child while worried about the other.

Every other day, I asked Malcolm if Patsy had called again, but he said she hadn't and refused to tell me where she was. I racked my brain, trying to figure out where she could be. I called hospitals, but they wouldn't tell me if Patsy was there. I was on the approved contact list for any time they admitted her, so either she wasn't there or had changed her approval list.

"Can I have this dance, my love?" Malcolm reached out his hand.

Though I didn't want to, I forced myself to dance with my husband.

"You look so beautiful in that red dress, sweetheart," he complimented me.

"Thank you. Remember, you have always felt that red is my color."

"It sure is." Malcolm gave me a spin. "I can't wait to take it off of you later."

"Oh, yeah?" I smiled. "Yes. I love you, Trish."

"I love you too, Malcolm. I always have."

"I always will," he finished.

As we danced, I felt worry-free in his arms . . . at least for the moment. I felt rested, comfortable, and safe. After the song ended, we separated and went in different directions, leaving me thinking,

My mind is tired. My heart is weary. My body is tired. I looked at my husband smiling at me from a distance. No matter how exhausted I was, my chief priority was being his wife. I vowed not to be like Carolyn or Lynette, alone at the end of the day.

CHAPTER FIFTEEN

For the following nights, my sleep was interrupted by vivid nightmares. I was alone in the dark in the dream when a figure appeared, struggling against a giant monster. I began to step forward, and the person's identity became clearer with each step.

Finally, my last step revealed it was Patsy. Her mouth was open in horror as he began to devour her. I reached out to Patsy, but she wouldn't take my hand. Instead, she backed farther and farther away from me into the monster.

"Come to Mama, Patsy. Come to Mama."

Patsy ignored me, walking backward until she was all but gone. "Don't do this, Patsy, please! I love you."

"I love you too, Mama," she said. "But I'm tired. I'm so tired." Then she was gone. The vile monster smiled at me with sharp, rabid teeth. In the dream, I fainted. In reality, I screamed, "No!" and bolted up in bed.

Sweat running across my forehead, my gown sticking to me, I groaned at the fact that I had another nightmare.

I placed my hand over my racing heart and tried to catch my breath. For a while, the nightmares had slowed down. Now, I have them every other night. I groped beside me, looking for Malcolm, but he wasn't there. I tossed my legs over the side of the bed, grabbed my robe, and threw it on.

I padded barefoot out of our room and headed down the dark hall. First, I checked in on the kids, who were sleeping peacefully.

Next, I had to find Malcolm. He wasn't in the living room or the kitchen. I checked upstairs, and he wasn't there, either. "Maybe he's outside," I yawned.

I checked the driveway, and he parked his truck in its usual place. Finally, I walked back through the house and found Malcolm sitting alone on the first step of our custom-built patio, staring up at the moon.

"Honey?"

Malcolm turned and peered at me. "Hey, baby. What are you doing up?"

"I had another nightmare. What are you doing out here?"

"I couldn't sleep, so I came out here to enjoy the stillness. Nature is amazing, isn't it? The moon, stars, and sky—we rarely sit still long enough to take in how beautiful they all are."

I stared up at the moon. "Remember that night in Japan?"

Malcolm chuckled. "How could I ever forget?"

We sat and watched the sky. "The moon was full, and the weather was nice," I reminisced.

Malcolm's soft chortle sailed through the air. "Yes, and you had a spontaneous moment."

"I sure did. A fenced-in backyard is for enjoying life outside. But I was on a mission."

"A mission that sent you to the hospital." Malcolm laughed loudly, no longer holding back.

I smiled. "Do you remember I'd set up a picnic outside for us that night?"

"Yes, I even remember that beautiful set of blankets and

pillows you made so we could have sex underneath the stars," he whispered. Then bursting into laughter, he said, "The evening was moving along as planned . . . until a raccoon came over the fence and wanted to be part of the show."

"I pleased you that night, all right. I was kissing you when a burning sensation suddenly brought me to reality. A raccoon had bitten me on the behind! After running and screaming, it attacked us both. You got rid of the raccoon and calmed me down. Then I forced you to rush me to the hospital to get a rabies shot and ensure I wouldn't get an infection."

"I have enjoyed doing life with you." Malcolm scooted me close to him. "It hasn't always been easy or happy, but it's been worth it. We've had a good life. Two teenagers from Decatur, Georgia, traveling all over the world with two babies, trying to figure life out as it came."

"I'm the luckiest woman in the world," I said. "You have always taken loving care of me. You saved me."

Malcolm nuzzled my nose. "And you saved me."

For a while, we sat there in peaceful silence. I couldn't be sure what Malcolm was thinking about, but the past thirty years of our life together came rushing back to me. First, our small wedding replayed in my head. Then our first anniversary as a married couple. Then his kiss when I gave birth to our daughter and his holding the video camera when I had MJ. Malcolm took my breath away in the moments when he was laughing. I got lucky. Yep, I sure did.

"Patsy's staying at a hotel right down the street," Malcolm whispered.

"What?" I exclaimed. "I've got to go to her. No, I *need* to get to her *now*!"

Malcolm grabbed my arm as I stood to run into the house.

"Hold on. She's right here close to home, Trish. And she's fine." I could barely contain my relief. Malcolm continued. "I don't know Patsy's room number, which doesn't bother her. Let her heal in her own way, honey. Give her the time and space she needs to figure out her next step. Let her figure out what's best for her and what she wants to do next."

Deflated, I sat. "As long as she's okay, I don't care what Patsy does. I just want her to be better and know she's safe and happy. That's it. The last thing I want is for my child to give up on herself or on life."

"Our girl's a fighter," Malcolm said. "She's doing what she needs to get healthy." He kissed my lips, then chuckled.

"Well, it's a full moon. You wanna…"

"Oh, heck no!" I stood up. "If you want this, come to the bedroom and get it. Remember the raccoon incident? Nothing's happening outside."

"Deal," Malcolm laughed. "I'll be there in a minute."

"Okay. Love you." "I know," he said.

CHAPTER SIXTEEN

Going back to work was bittersweet. I had been out for two weeks looking for Patsy. Upon my arrival, I was shocked to realize this was my work friend Lynette's last day at the company. Watching Lynette pack up her desk, I suspected I wouldn't see or hear from her in the future.

Her life was about to change forever; I was afraid of becoming the friend she used to work with, whom she only called on birthdays and holidays. Losing my two closest friends in such a short amount of time stung. Of course, Carolyn called at least once a day and I missed her, but how could I forgive her for betraying my family? These feelings of loneliness and betrayal had me out of sorts. With a tightness in my chest, I said goodbye to Lynette and left work a little early. I wanted to get home and take a nap before Malcolm got home after picking up the kids.

But when I pulled into the driveway of my home, I saw a strange car parked out front. The man driving the vehicle was Asian. "May I help you?" I asked, approaching the vehicle.

Hardly understanding his response, I translated it as, "I'm waiting for the lady to return. She told me to wait out here for thirty minutes."

As soon as he told me, the front door flew open.

"Patsy?" "Mama!" she said.

I dropped my work bag and purse and ran to her. "Patsy!"

"Hey, Mama." The sound of her laughter was like an ointment to my soul.

Frantically, I touched her all over and examined her. She looked better. The bruises healed, and she appeared clean.

"You're off early," Patsy said. "I've been coming here every day when no one is here. I sit for a while to feel close to you."

"Oh, baby, come home."

"I don't know when I'll come home, Mama, but I'm working hard to get better. I want to be a wonderful mother to my children." She pecked my cheek and squeezed me. "I'll see you later."

"Please don't go, baby. Stay here, where you're safe, and I can protect you."

"I'm safe where I am, Mama. But I need a controlled environment to ensure I take my meditation as prescribed so I can't harm myself or anyone else."

She rushed across the yard and got into the car's backseat. Patsy grinned as the car pulled out of the driveway and sped down the street.

As soon as she was out of sight, I cried. I missed my sweet girl so much, but laying eyes on her eased the pain and gave me a bit of relief. I rushed to pick up my dropped items when I first saw Patsy. After running into the house, I phoned Malcolm and told him the news.

"Patsy was here, Malcolm! I saw her. She looked good, as though she was okay. Her hair was clean and neat, her skin glowed, and her eyes sparkled. Her dress fit her small body, and her shoes matched her dress. She looked like her old self. I now have hope that Patsy will make a full recovery. I'm encouraged that she will fully function in society and take care of her children and her household without experiencing these episodes. Malcolm, I'm so happy."

"That's a positive report, Trish. That means Patsy *is* healing. But slow it down, okay?"

"Why? I finally have hope. Based on what I saw, Patsy should come home soon. I understand she needs to do it in her time, but I'm so ready for all this to end."

Malcolm and I talked for one or two more minutes about Patsy's health before he had to go back to work.

CHAPTER SEVENTEEN

What is it, Carolyn?" I reluctantly answered her call after ignoring the other five. There was silence, then a stutter.

"C- can we talk?"

"No."

"Please, I miss my friend."

"Friend? Was I *ever* your friend?"

"Of course, you were. You still are." "Well,   friend, why wasn't our friendship important enough to keep you from having an affair with my daughter's husband?"

"It was a terrible mistake."

"A mistake my daughter had to pay for."

"Haven't you ever done anything that you regret?" Carolyn asked.

I held the phone away from me. I wanted to hang up but answered her question.

"Hurt someone that caused irreparable harm? You know you were wrong and shouldn't do it, but you did it anyway. Remember, I'm your best friend. I know you. You couldn't even give me a real reason that you would bring my husband's biggest mistake into the place I call my holy sanctuary. Jealous? You know enough about my pain *not* to envy my life. And yet, you want *me* to choose forgiveness."

"Your holy place? It's where *I* worship too. And while you know me, I also know you," Carolyn sneered. "Your hands aren't so clean from jealous maneuvers. Why can't you give grace when grace is needed?"

I knew what Carolyn was referring to and I wasn't proud of my actions and didn't ask for forgiveness when I did dirt that I didn't feel I should be forgiven for, especially when my dirt was premeditated. For example, I'm responsible for my sister's divorce. I told her husband she was cheating on him because my sister—Georgine— always thought and even said she was better than everyone, especially me. She reminded me of Mama. She was as evil as Mama was too. So, I told him. But I suffered after I saw how hurt she was by the divorce. She experienced an awful stage of depression. She thought her husband, Nick, was the best thing ever for her, and she acted like she couldn't live without him. I still don't understand why she jeopardized their union for a fling.

So often, I thought about telling Georgine about what I'd done and asking for her forgiveness, but somehow, I could never confess. We'd never had a good relationship, and now that we were on decent terms, I didn't see the point in making things worse than they'd ever been.

Another thing I needed forgiveness for happened years ago. I'd purposely got an old coworker fired so that I could replace her, knowing she had small kids at home. But she was lazy and I was better at the job than her. I felt like I deserved her position . . . so I took it.

I wasn't proud of my wrongs, but at least I hadn't slept with someone else's husband. Even when I thought about getting even with Malcolm, the man I'd planned to cheat with was single. Thinking back on all my past deeds, I knew Carolyn deserved forgiveness. We all do. I just wasn't ready yet.

"How often do I have to apologize, Trish?"

"Until I believe you." I then hung up on her and blocked her number.

Forgiveness isn't a joke or a game. Or is it? It could be a game that we repeatedly play throughout life. Sometimes we win and sometimes we lose. But we always play. Unfortunately, we all experience loss, betrayal. and pain. Forgiveness was a turnstile that we all needed to go through again and again if we wanted to get to the other side. Peace.

Once Patsy was home and doing better, I'd forgive my friend and move past her betrayal. But God forbid if any harm came to Patsy—if one of my nightmares came true—I'd never forgive Carolyn or Bounce.

Never.

CHAPTER EIGHTEEN

The phone rang as soon as I blocked Carolyn. I checked the caller ID to ensure she wasn't trying to call me from a private number.

"Hey, son!" I tried sounding more cheerful than I felt.

"They're shipping me out," MJ muttered.

I've always hated those words. "Where?"

"Kuwait."

I listened while MJ laid out the details. He then revealed he wanted to get married before leaving and wanted his father and me to witness it. Since he was short on time, I convinced him to marry at the courthouse and let me plan a small, intimate reception. I wanted Clara to wear a beautiful dress and feel love and admiration, even for an hour or two. Every woman deserves her moment.

My moment was over so fast that I barely remembered our vows. I'm not sure I meant them back then, but now, our vows mean more to me. There was nothing I wouldn't do for my husband and I loved him with all my being. It was terrific knowing he reciprocated my feelings.

I never got to take that nap. Instead, I talked to my son until it was time to pick up my grandbabies.

When I arrived at the school, I met one of Malcolm's

coworkers, Eugene. Like me, I often met him picking up his grandkids. After the usual pleasantries, he asked, "How's Malcolm feeling?"

"He's fine." I was curious why Eugene asked about Malcolm's health.

"Good." Eugene looked relieved. "Malcolm got out of there so fast this morning I didn't have time to speak to him."

"He got out of where?"

"Work. He said he didn't feel well."

Two hours ago, Malcolm told me he was still in the office. One teacher helped get William's things together and helped him get ready to leave. Paige and Sophie were waiting at the car.

Then, after the usual goodbyes, I got the kids in the car and hurriedly called Malcolm.

"Hi," Malcolm cheerfully greeted me. "Where are you?"

"I'm at home."

"Where have you been?" "What do you mean?"

"I ran into Eugene. He told me you left work early. Why didn't you tell me that when I spoke to you? Where have you been?"

"I wasn't feeling well."

"Then why did you pretend to be at work when I called you?"

"You were already in an uproar about Patsy, Trish. So, I didn't want to worry you."

"Worry me about what?" "About me not feeling well."

"What? You know that sounds ridiculous, right?" I scowled into the phone. "You are my *husband*, Malcolm. I'm supposed to *know* if you're not feeling well. You also need to tell me when you leave work early. So, tell me, what's going on?"

"It's nothing to worry about, Trish." "What's not to worry about?"

"I'll tell you later. I'll see you when you get here." Malcolm hung up without saying goodbye.

Ending that strange conversation, I headed home. I had planned to go to the grocery store, but I wanted to talk to Malcolm. Knowing the kids would happily have pizza for dinner, I hurried home.

Reflecting on Malcolm's caginess, I decided that if I found Malcolm with another woman when I got home, I would shoot them, no questions asked. I added their murders to Bounce's.

After his affair, it took me a while to trust Malcolm again, but I fought to keep his attention. I made sure I was home whenever he was. Our weekly date nights were legendary. We planned exciting and different dates for every Friday night. Sometimes, we even splurged on a three-day weekend if we didn't have children duty.

Even though we were together during nonwork hours, I tracked his whereabouts and called him when he was gone longer than I felt necessary. And God forbid if he missed one of my calls—I went crazy, accusing him of being where he wasn't and doing what he wasn't, then convinced myself he wasn't coming back home. It was rough.

I never wanted to experience that again. And if Malcolm loved me, he wouldn't put me in that situation again.

When I arrived home and got the kids settled, I found Malcolm on the patio smoking a cigar.

"What's going on?" "I'm fine, Trish."

"Why did you leave work?"

"Oh, I was serious about not being well."

"Then what's wrong that you can't tell me?"

"You have enough to worry about right now. I don't want to add any more worry or stress. Be at peace, baby."

I stared at my husband without blinking, wondering why he had a smile on his face.

"What are you not telling me?" Malcolm took another puff from his cigar.

"Tell me."

"Tell you what?" "Malcolm, I'm serious!"

"And I'm serious too. Go on and get

the kids fed and settled."

I could tell the conversation was over. Malcolm wasn't telling me what he knew. I needed to be more knowledgeable about what he was up to.

My mind was frantic. Patsy still had yet to return home, MJ was on his way to Kuwait, and Carolyn proved she was never my friend. Now my love was acting mysterious and cagey. Why were all my bridges burning down?

"I love you, Trish."

I traipsed down the hall to call for the pizza delivery, calling over my shoulder, "For your sake, you better."

CHAPTER NINETEEN

I rose early the next day and went into the kitchen to cook everyone's breakfast. We were going to church and I didn't want my grandbabies complaining that they were hungry in Sunday school.

Kids will embarrass you if you let them. I filled a pot with water for grits, sprinkled a teaspoon of salt in it, and set it on the eye to boil. Humming while I moved about the kitchen, I mentally sorted through the mess that had become my life.

I figured Bounce must have been back in town because I'd seen his truck darting around town. He hadn't tried to pick up the kids. And for his sake, he better not come near my house, or I'm shooting him for real.

Whenever I saw him, I wondered if Patsy was in the passenger seat. Or if Carolyn was riding with him. After I blocked Carolyn's original phone number, she tried calling me from different numbers and leaving multiple messages. Eventually, she stopped calling. I'd be lying if I said I didn't miss her. Carolyn had a sense of humor that I gloried in. But now that she was gone, I had no one to vent to without judging me. I missed her presence but not enough to forgive her.

I cracked eggs into a bowl and whisked them like I had a vendetta against the chicken who hatched them. As I poured the eggs into the pan, the bacon had just started sizzling in the skillet. As I added butter to the grits, I heard the patter of feet, and Malcolm cautioned the kids to stop running in the hallway and wash their hands.

"Morning, love," I said as Malcolm strolled into the kitchen, stretching.

He poured himself a cup of coffee and half-sat on the bar stool. "Good morning, yourself. You tossed and turned excessively last night. Are you well?"

"Uh-huh," I said and started plating everyone's food.

Malcolm nodded, then ushered the kids to the table and put their plates in front of them. I followed behind with our breakfast. He and I locked eyes knowing this would be our new normal for the unforeseen future.

"Hey." He bumped me teasingly on the shoulder.

"How are you feeling?"

"Hungry." Malcolm smiled, then kissed me. Being married to Malcolm was a journey. Our life was one adventure after another, but we loved, fought, and survived through it all. We finished breakfast and went on with our day.

Monday started just like any other work/school day. We got the kids ready for school, Malcolm went to work, and I dropped them off at day care. The girls would walk to school and the day care provider would take and pick up William. In the afternoons, the girls would pick up William and they would all wait at the day care for Malcolm or myself to come get them. But today, when I got there, they were already gone.

"What do you mean they're gone? You mean my husband came to get them?" I asked the center receptionist.

"No," she said, "their father picked them up," the little gum-popping secretary stated flippantly.

I stormed out, dialing Bounce's cell number, but he didn't answer. I'd gone to pick up my grandbabies, and without a hello and thank you, he just picked them up and dashed away. No respect. He could have had the common decency to text and inform me he was picking them up today. This man was playing dangerously with his God-given grace. Even though I had custody of the children, I never opposed Bounce spending time with them. Since Patsy needed hospitalization frequently, it was easier not to have to do temporary custody paperwork each time.

Bounce and Patsy signed a custody agreement when she was hospitalized for over a month a year ago. We had to find Bounce when William fell while riding his bike and broke his arm. The hospital needed someone with legal custody to sign the paperwork. I always kept that document with me. Although Bounce was still allowed to pick them up, someone at the school should have notified me. Someone dropped the ball. They would hear about it later.

Lord, what's next when my grace for Bounce has run out?

Mine hasn't run out for you.

I wasn't trying to hear God right then. He had a particular habit of pressing into my spirit when I least wanted to hear from Him. I needed to be angry right now.

I frantically redialed Bounce. "Answer the phone," I screamed at his voicemail. I called him back-to-back for ten minutes straight until he blocked my number. Then finally, I pulled up at his and Patsy's house. Seeing that no one was home, a horrible feeling consumed me. What if I never saw my grandbabies again? I called Malcolm to tell him what was going on. "The kids are gone!"

"What do you mean the kids are gone?"

I struggled to catch my breath.

"Bounce picked up the kids before I got there. When I spoke to the secretary she said that their father picked them up like he's done in the past." I didn't understand why they said that because the supervisor had our custody documentation on file. Bounce's name was also on the permission to pick up, but he rarely used it. Malcolm and I dropped the kids off and picked them up more than Bounce did.

"Well, Trish, he *is* their father," Malcolm sighed.

"I don't care. They're Patsy's kids too! And we have custody of them."

"Yes, but Patsy isn't the one taking care of them. We are." Malcolm spoke with such infuriating calm.

"Exactly. They are our daughter's children, and she wants *us* to look after them until she feels better. Bounce had no right to go up there and just take them." My voice shook. I was livid. "What if he moves away with them? What if we never see them again?"

"Trish, honey, breathe," Malcolm soothed me. "Bounce loves those kids. He won't harm them. He missed them, and I'm sure he's ready for them to come home, Trish. And—"

"And what?" "Nothing."

"What is it, Malcolm?"

"Nothing. Are you on your way home?"

"Yes, I'll be there soon."

But instead of going straight home like I told him I would, I drove around for hours, looking for Bounce's truck, scanning every hotel parking lot I could think of, and driving by his family members' homes. I even swung by Bounce's dealership to see if he was there. I was anxious because I couldn't reach him on my phone. My grandkids didn't need to be part of the mess adults created.

Five frantic hours later, I finally arrived home. I tossed my keys in the bowl by our entryway, hesitating before going to the den and sitting in front of Malcolm because I knew he disapproved of my actions.

"Did you find them?"

I looked everywhere but at him.

"No."

"Good."

"What do you mean good?" I shrieked. "They're our *grandkids*, and they're with Bounce!"

Malcolm swiped a hand down his face. Frustration ran both ways. "I said they're with their father."

"What's going on with you?" I asked, standing up with sudden sharp pangs in my chest, "Trish."

"Trish, sit back down." I shook my head.

He took a deep breath. "I'm dying, I stumbled into the chair. "What?" Solemnly, Malcolm folded his hand in his lap. "I went for a doctor's appointment. He said I have three to six months to live . . .if that."

I was at a loss for words. The pangs I felt earlier pulsated even faster. My heart was breaking, and I couldn't do anything to gather the pieces back together.

Malcolm said softly, "Stage four prostate cancer. It's aggressive. There's nothing they can do about it. I found out right after all this mess with Patsy started going on. That day I left work early I went to have additional tests. There's nothing they can do. I'm dying, and I just want to spend the rest of my days doing everything I've ever wanted to do. And I want to do them with you." He exhaled. "We can't do those things with the kids. They should be with their father. They don't need you right now, Trish. I do."

I cried and wrapped my arms around my husband's neck. "Oh, Malcolm," I sobbed. "Why did you wait so long to visit the doctor? Regardless of whether you had symptoms, you know it's the Black man's killer."

I quoted statistics he already knew. "One in six Black men will develop prostate cancer in his lifetime. You know your father died of it at fifty-five. You told me you were getting your screenings. Haven't you been getting your annual physical?"

I continued with my tirade. "It's my fault. I didn't give you the attention you needed. I was too busy with Patsy and the grandchildren. You are more important to me than any of them." I fell on my knees, wrapped myself around his legs, and moaned, "I promised to take care of you through sickness and health. I failed God and I failed you. But I am with you, no matter what."

Like Jesus, I wept.

CHAPTER TWENTY

Patsy?" I shouted. It had been a hard night, and I woke up exhausted. My daughter was sitting at the kitchen table when I wandered into the kitchen.

"Sorry. I've been here for a while. I didn't want to wake you."

I hugged her, then looked her over. "You look good."

"I feel good, Mama."

I took a seat in front of her at the table. "Bounce has the kids," I said to her. She shrugged. "I know."

"You've spoken to him?" "Yes."

"Are the kids, okay?"

Patsy rolled her eyes. "Of course they are. He loves our kids. He wouldn't do anything to hurt them."

"He loves you too and we see how that turned out."

"Good point," she mumbled.

I scrutinized her with a hard stare. Patsy's shine could have been brighter. It wasn't that it was dim. It was more a look of contentment. I found her beautiful. Her new hairstyle accentuated her face, and she wore less makeup than usual. She looked like she was at peace. Even, dare I hope, she was ready to return home.

"Are you going back to Bounce?" "Yes." Patsy looked away.

"But I thought—"

"I'm damaged goods, Mama. Bounce knows all of me. He knows what I'm dealing with."

I spoke low and firm, trying to get through to her. "But he hits you."

Patsy looked me square in the face. "I hit him too."

"It's not the same, Patsy."

"I know, but only because he hits back harder."

I shouldn't have offered after last night and Malcolm's revelation concerning his health, but I couldn't help it. "You can stay here with us. You don't have to go back."

Patsy shook her head. "I'm giving my marriage another chance."

"What does Bounce have to do—hit you again? Cheat on you with Carolyn again?"

Patsy drew in a hard breath. "You know about Bounce and Carolyn?"

"Isn't that what the fight was about— because you found out about them?"

"No. Bounce told me about it from the beginning. We fought because I didn't take my meds. I started having a manic episode. When that happens, I can't stop myself. I get so hyped, that people think I'm on drugs, but Bounce knows me. He asked me to take my meds, and I refused, thinking I didn't need them. I was bopping around the house and rushing and screaming at the kids to do chores they had already completed and he brought my meds and asked me to take them. I threw them at him. He told the kids to leave the room. He then cut up the volume of the TV in their room."

Wringing her hands, Patsy searched my face for my reaction. "He's had to do it before."

I tried to understand all that had been happening right under my nose. "Why didn't you take your medication? You know what happens when you don't." I tried reaching for Patsy's hand, but she snatched it away. I sat back and bit my lip.

"All the meds they've ever put me on keep me in a fog. How would you like to live your life inside a dark cloud? Remember the little Black boy—Pigpen, in the Charlie Brown cartoons? Well, my cloud isn't over my head. It lives inside me. And when schizophrenia kicks in, people are in the cloud, crowding me. Different ones are aggressive, and a small group is meek, but they're all vying for my attention."

Patsy stood and paced the room. "You've never understood. You act like I have control over my actions, but I don't. I never have. Bounce gets that, but he gets discouraged."

Stopping and staring at me, she continued. "When I refuse to take my meds, he tries forcing me to take them, which leads to me hitting him. Lately, he's returning those hits harder and longer, resulting in bruises all over my body. And then there's the other thing. I broke our code."

"What code?"

Slowly, with her head down, Patsy attempted to explain. "I knew Carolyn and Bounce were sleeping together."

With my hands on my hips, I screamed, "What?! You *knew* your husband was cheating on you?"

Nodding her head, Patsy continued. "But Bounce and I got into a volatile fight because he found out—" Patsy paused and looked away. Tears flooded her eyes as she shared, "Bounce and I both have had others outside of our marriage. It works for us. Well, at least it used to."

Feeling floored, I asked, "You think it was okay to be a

swinger, Patsy?"

"Yes, Mama. Try to understand. We always let each other know who we're sleeping with. I introduced the idea to him. But, Mom, you know I'm not myself if I'm off my meds." Tears flowed down her face. "When I'm someone else—I call her Francesco—she wants to do other things with other people," Patsy said, holding her hands in the air, "Bounce understood and accepted that about me. We had one rule: never fall in love. We would only ever love each other."

I grabbed my chest and gasped. "You and Bounce were swingers? You knowingly had sexual relations with other husbands and wives?"

"Yes, Mama, you could say that. When I sought thrills," Patsy said, "it's what I found to do. We were always honest, and I didn't stray without telling Bounce. He always did the same."

My mouth hit the floor. "Y'all have an open marriage?" I asked again with unbelief.

"I admit it. That's what we had."

"I raised you better than that, baby." "It has nothing to do with how you raised me, Mama. This is how things work inside my head."

I didn't know whether to feel sorry for her or disappointed. "You knew Bounce was fooling around with Carolyn?"

Patsy nodded. "He asked me if it was okay. He said she seemed lonely and desperate. I told him she was. Guess I was right."

My mouth hung wide open. "Why did Bounce beat you the way he did?" I screeched.

Patsy was silent.

"For God's sake, Patsy, your husband almost killed you!

Why would he do that to you?"

Patsy took a deep breath. "Mom, he snapped. The things I asked and needed him to do can sometimes be expansive, but he's always come through for me—always! Because he loves me. He's been with me through my worst and held my hand through my lowest points."

"Even before I would have him call you, Bounce was right there. I made a mistake. We agreed to protect ourselves and tested for diseases regularly. We were to keep our medical records on us and request our partners verify theirs before having relations with them."

Feeling faint, I plopped down into the nearest chair, trying to comprehend what my child had told me.

"Somewhere along the line, I slipped up." Patsy dried the tears welling in her eyes and wrung her hands. "Bounce beat me because he found out he's HIV positive and got it from me."

"What?" I shot from the chair.

"He was upset, hurt, and scared. He has every right to be angry."

"You have HIV?"

"Yes, I do. That's why I stayed so long at the facility. The doctors had to adjust my HIV cocktail with my mental health drugs. But Bounce has forgiven me. He still loves me, and he wants to make our marriage work. He wants me to come home."

"Patsy, baby, I just don't know what to say."

"Just say you love me, Mama. That's all I need to hear."

"I love you."

"I love you too." Patsy stood to her feet.

"Patsy?"

"Yes, Mama?"

"Do you know who gave you HIV?" "Yes, Mama."

"Who?"

Patsy opened the front door. She didn't bother looking back at me as she spoke. "Pastor Troy gave it to me."

Jesus! Not my pastor!

CHAPTER TWENTY-ONE

The following week, I stopped at the grocery store on my way home from work. While getting out of the car and grabbing a cart in the store's parking lot, I headed to the entrance when I heard,

"Trish?" I turned around to face Dianna, Malcolm's ex-mistress.

"I was hoping to speak with you after church the other week, but you left before the service ended," Dianna hurriedly explained.

All I noticed was how gorgeous she was as she approached me. "Talk to me about what?" I snapped.

Although her voice was shaky and apprehensive, Dianna looked me in the eye. "I just wanted to apologize face-to-face. I'm so sorry for my role in the affair with your husband. Please forgive me." Dianna's voice became more assertive as she attempted to explain herself.

"When I met your friend, Carolyn, she sat alone on a park bench. I didn't know she was your friend. I just saw a lady crying and reached out to her. She knew who I was. She called me by name and loudly accused me of sleeping with her best friend's husband. And then she sobbed again."

I turned away from Dianna, but she kept talking to me.

"She told me there's an issue between the two of you but didn't go into detail. She said she wasn't sure if you would ever forgive her. I'd wanted to know the same thing. We all make mistakes. We all deserve forgiveness. I never knew who you were. I knew Malcolm was married, but he never even told me your name. And for that, I am sorry. Carolyn told me the two of you went to the same church, so I asked her if I could go as her guest to speak with you. Again, I am sorry for what I did and I hope that someday you can find it in your heart to forgive me."

I stood there rigid with remembered pain. I wanted her gone, but she continued talking as though she couldn't see my face drained of all color. Meeting her like this was a nightmare I prayed would never come true.

"I know coming to you like this seems out of the ordinary. But I'm engaged. I'm getting married. Thinking about the effect of an affair on my marriage, I understand what I did and hope the same thing doesn't happen to me as a wife."

Then I saw a sparkle on her ring finger. *Karma doesn't feel good, but what you sow, you will harvest.*

Honestly, I should forgive her because I forgave Malcolm long ago. It's only right to forgive her too. She didn't cheat on me. He did. Until now, I didn't think she wanted my forgiveness or cared about it.

Realizing what I needed to do, I looked her in the eye and said, "I forgive you." We hugged, and I felt lighter while letting go of that root of bitterness.

"Thank you so much," she said. "This means so much to me."

With that, she smiled and walked away. I said nothing more. I didn't know what else to say. I watched until she disappeared.

With Dianna no longer in sight, I rushed into the grocery store to grab what I needed to cook Malcolm's favorite dinner: turkey necks, rice, gravy, and cornbread. Since he told me about his diagnosis, I'd been spoiling and loving him as much as possible. I thought we had about twenty years left together, at least. Knowing how fast we lost time was destroying me.

Malcolm was important to me. I couldn't shoulder all these burdens alone. I wasn't ready to bury my husband.

While shopping, I thought about how paranoid I'd become about Patsy since she moved back home with Bounce. I have been obsessed with constantly calling and checking up on her for a while. I wanted to know her every move from when she woke up in the morning until I laid my head to rest at night.

"She's got this," I kept telling myself. I despised that adultery had turned Patsy's life into the mess it was. Now, she had to live with her poor decisions as long as she lived.

My line of thinking led me to thoughts of Pastor Troy. The pastor I once loved and followed, I now hated and he hated me too.

At church the following Sunday, I stood and exposed him in front of his wife and congregation during testimony time.

Dressed to impress, I stood with my head up and my back straight. "Our beloved pastor, the one who encourages his members to be faithful to our spouses . . ."

"Amen!" the congregation chimed.

I cleared my throat and spoke louder. "Our pastor, who conducts marriage counseling and retreats, the one we hold as our leader above reproach, the pastor who warns us to be aware of Satan tempting us with sex and power . . ."

Everyone jumped to their feet, including Pastor Troy,

shouting in agreement.

"Well, you need to know he was unfaithful to his wife, all while standing in the pulpit every Sunday, preaching salvation. The same man who told you sin is wrong has infected a member of this church with HIV. Our illustrious Pastor Troy!" I spat out my story with venom without mentioning Patsy's name.

Pastor Troy nearly choked as he scanned the stunned faces of the congregation. Everyone rumbled, wondering aloud if what I said was true.

Pastor Troy looked at his wife, who repeatedly wailed, "Why?" Then, she looked at him and asked, "Are *you* the reason I have HIV? I told the doctors they had to keep searching to determine how I contracted it. I told them there was no way I got it from you because you were faithful to your church members and me. You would never hurt any of us."

People around the first lady thinned out as spital flew from her mouth as she screamed at her husband. Two other female members cried, "Lord, please don't let him have given it to me." Shocked, the first lady ran shrieking from the sanctuary.

Finally, Pastor Troy bolted to the front and grabbed the microphone. "Let those without sin cast the first stone," he bellowed. "Please, forgive me—I have sinned." Then he raced from the pulpit after his wife.

Since that day, I haven't returned to the church and wasn't sure I'd ever step back inside it again. Church hurt is different; it stings worse than betrayal. It's like a rape unreported because no one would believe it. Half of those folks sneered at me on the way out of the sanctuary. They were of the persuasion that God's call on a man could do no wrong and thought I should not have exposed him.

I drove home in silence. Although I don't socialize with the ones who stayed, the other half left "Standing on the Rock Church" right along with me.

CHAPTER TWENTY-TWO

The following weekend, Malcolm and I were supposed to make the trip to witness MJ get married before he shipped out. But unfortunately, because so much was happening, we canceled the ceremony and held the reception instead. MJ's assignment was for two years. Too long for me not to see my son.

I called Patsy and tried to convince her to come along with us, but she said she'd wait until the big wedding, whenever that would be.

I remembered our brief call just this morning. I wasn't sure what was happening, but I needed to focus on Malcolm now. "Hey, baby. How are you holding up? What are the kids up to?"

"They're playing," Patsy said dryly. "Are you okay, baby?" I questioned. "Yes, ma'am."

I knew she was lying but decided not to badger her. "Okay, well, I'll call you back later."

"Okay," she whispered.

As we hung up, the doorbell rang, and I went to answer it. Daddy was standing outside.

"Why haven't you been answering my calls?" he demanded when I opened the door.

"You and I both know why." I walked away as soon as he

was inside.

"Anger looks so ugly on you." Daddy slammed the door behind him.

I jammed my hands on my hips. "You would know, wouldn't you?"

"Trish, let's squash this between us. I was out of line with what I said, and I'm sorry. Now, can we move past it all?"

I didn't know why forgiveness had been so hard for me lately, but it was. I sighed as though the world was on my shoulders and the weight was too heavy to carry.

"I'm cooking. Stay for dinner."

That's all the forgiveness he would get from me for the moment. Daddy found Malcolm in the living room. I went out the back door for fresh air while they waited for me to prepare the food. I stood under the enormous maple tree in our backyard. My ritual was to gaze at it whenever I felt overwhelmed. It brought me peace. There was something about its majestic countenance, with its broad, wide branches covering me like God was spreading his wings just for us. I needed to remind myself of this most days. Inhaling one more time before I went inside to check my dinner, I turned the doorknob and opened the door. Then I heard Malcolm shouting, "Trish! Call 911!"

"I'm coming—" I frantically called back when he yelled again. "I think your father's having a heart attack."

~~~~

The group Boyz II Men knew my heart when they sang, "It's So Hard to Say Goodbye to Yesterday." The Homegoing Celebration for Daddy was the following week. While peering
~~~~

into Daddy's stoic face for the last time at his funeral, I noticed a fresh crop of wrinkles tracing across his forehead as though he were in deep thought. He used to get those same lines when he was mad or found what we said funny. I wonder which one was his last thought. I hated that I would not be able to talk to him. We buried him in the church cemetery next to Mama. As the funeral home attendants lowered Daddy's coffin into the ground at the grave site, I thought about the day we buried Mama.

Mama's funeral was on a cold, rainy day, completely the opposite of today. She was wearing a pale blue dress and pearls. I wasn't fond of the wig my sister Bebe had chosen for her to wear, but since she was the oldest, she handled the funeral arrangements.

I remember staring at Mama's face. It was relaxed like she was at peace. She'd raised all that hell while alive and well; now, she was finally quiet. And I didn't shed a tear.

Then my heart began to soften.
"Goodbye, Daddy. I forgive you."
Finally, I felt at peace with my father. I didn't know what took me so long to forgive him, but I'm thankful I let go of my bitterness toward him.

While I was there reminiscing about Mama, Patsy approached me and asked, "How are you holding up, Mama?"

"I'm good, Patsy. Are you? I noticed your family did not come."

Patsy had come to the funeral without Bounce or the kids. She nodded. Briefly, I scanned her body from head to toe. She looked good, dressed in black, a hat, and three-inch heels. I saw no physical marks.

"I can't believe Grandpa is gone," she whispered. "I'm going to miss him."

"Me too."

"He was a mess, wasn't he?" Patsy said.

"He sure was."

"He told me that the two of you were arguing about what happened to me. That's why I encouraged him to visit you." Patsy smiled. "I'm glad you had one last conversation before it was time for him to go."

"You talked to your grandpa?"

Patsy nodded. "Who do you think paid for the hotel the whole time I was there?"

"Daddy did that? He *knew* where you were?"

"No questions asked," she confirmed.

"He said he would do anything to keep me safe and help me get back to where I needed to be."

Why didn't I accept any of his calls so he could tell me that?

Breaking into my thoughts, Patsy announced, "Bounce wants to make things right. He wants to sit down and talk with you and Daddy."

"Patsy, I'm not ready for that." "When you are, let me know."

Frowning, I said, "I don't want to bury you next." I hadn't meant to say the words. They simply slipped out.

"I'm not going anywhere. I have three kids to live for, and that's precisely what I will do. God can get our attention and shut us down when He needs to. But he has a way of making our crooked paths straight. I'm a work in progress. God is working on me. He hasn't given up on me. I'm learning my lessons and holding myself accountable for my mistakes. The best for me is yet to come."

At that moment, I wanted to tell Patsy about her father and unburden my load to someone to help me carry it. But I wasn't sure how she'd react to losing her father. In the past, Pasty didn't handle negative information well. She would get upset, resulting in a mental meltdown.

For that reason, Malcolm and I kept the news of his cancer away from the kids, though we didn't have long to tell them. His oncologist said because of the aggressiveness of his cancer, it had spread throughout his body. His life expectancy was measured in months. So we had to decide if telling her before or waiting until he passed would traumatize her the most. Either way, I could only pray that it didn't cause her to spiral out of control.

We decided we would say nothing before MJ's wedding. We wanted to maintain the sovereignty of his special occasion. Because knowing my son the way I do, he would postpone the entire event to spend his daddy's last days with him.

The drive home from the burial was a sad one. I cried until my eyes were sore. Malcolm said sweet and encouraging words, none of which helped me feel better.

My father was gone.

. . . And my husband was next.

"Trust, sweetheart. All will be good when this is over."

"You always say that, but it's a lie! Soon, it'll be *your* grave that I'm standing over. I'm not ready for that, Malcolm."

Malcolm pulled into our driveway and parked the car. He unbuckled his seat belt, pulled me close, and held me in his arms. "I will always be with you and watching over you, Trish. You can't get rid of me, woman. Do you hear me? I will be gone in the physical, but I'll always be right here with you."

My future flashed before my eyes, coming home to our big empty house. Malcolm was gone, and the kids did notneed me anymore. We were happy to be empty nesters. Now, what am I? So, life is the same boring episode, playing repeatedly.

As if he could read my mind, Malcolm mumbled, "I need a promise from you, Trish. When I go, don't stop living. You understand? I want you to enjoy life and do all the things that we never got around to doing. Promise me you will continue to travel to all the places on our list and that you'll try all the crazy foods we planned on eating. Promise me you won't sit in this house and rot away. You will live and be happy. Promise me."

Taking in what he said, I realized I'd be like Lynette: no husband or kids to tend to. I could travel with her. Not knowing when my last day with Malcolm would be was torture.

"Promise me, Trish," he repeated.

I wiped my eyes and smiled just for him. "I promise."

CHAPTER TWENTY-THREE

For the next week, I was a complete mess. I prayed without ceasing, asking God for healing, restoration, forgiveness, and understanding. I begged for my husband and daughter on my behalf, asking God to keep them safe and alive with me. I felt God would respond to my prayers if I did my part. Then it occurred to me that God did not hear my prayers based on scripture. I still had unforgiveness in my heart. So, I went to His word, and I couldn't believe all the ways He instructed me to forgive.

Mark 11:25, where He told me that if I want to pray to Him, my Father, I should first forgive so He can forgive me. *Lord, forgive me.*

Matthew 14–15, where He tells me that I should forgive others so He may forgive me. *Lord, forgive me.*

Ephesians 4:32, where He commands me to be kind and tenderhearted, forgiving one another, as He has forgiven me. *Lord, forgive me.*

And so many more scriptures go on and on, repeatedly saying that I cannot expect God to forgive me when I have not forgiven others.

I was fearful my months of disobedience would result in God not hearing my prayers. I felt convicted down to my small size six feet. I had to act.

Realizing that I needed to ask Carolyn to forgive me for how I treated her, I went to her house. When I got there, she wasn't home. Instead, her neighbor told me she'd packed up her things and moved to Tennessee, where her family was.

Sitting on her front porch steps, I unblocked her phone number and tried to call her but found the number disconnected. I'd never get the chance to tell her I forgave her or, more importantly, ask her to forgive me. Why did I have to be so stubborn? Why had I allowed Satan to put blinders on my eyes and harden my heart?

"You're strong, and you'll get through this," I told myself. "I'm not sure how, but I will."

Still sitting on Carolyn's porch, I felt dejected and needed someone to talk to. Since I couldn't talk to Carolyn and hadn't told the kids about Malcolm, I had to tell someone. I decided to call my other best friend, Lynette. I located her number in my phone and called her as I left Carolyn's house.

She recognized my number and said, "Hey, Trish, how's it going?" when she answered the phone.

"Today hasn't been a good day." "I heard about your dad."

"Yes, he's gone."

"Seriously, how are you holding on with all that's been happening lately?"

"I don't know the answer to that question," I said tearfully.

Hearing the pain in my voice, she asked, "How can I help?"

Feeling distraught, I spilled, "Malcolm has stage four prostate cancer. He's dying." I then broke down sobbing. "He only has four months to live."

"Oh, no, Trish. I'm sorry to hear that.

Do you need me to come over?"

"No, I just need to talk it out. It's hard for me to accept it."

"I understand. The two of you are so perfect together," Lynette said. "I don't know how to help except to say I'll be praying for you."

"Please do. My family needs your prayers, and I believe in its power." The phone was then quiet. Lynette didn't know what to say, and I now felt I should have kept this to myself. "So what about you? How are things going?" I managed to ask, trying to be polite while experiencing chaos.

"Honestly, it's taken time to adjust to my new life. There are days when my life is quiet and still. That's when I miss my husband . . . but only for a second. I miss the familiarity of a marriage relationship. But then, when I participate in an exciting event, that feeling disappears. I believe I made the best decision for me."

"Good. So, where are you off to next?"

"I'll be going to Cabo soon. I know you are busy with your husband and daughter right now, but if you want to get away, let me know, and I'll take you with me."

"Thank you, my friend. I pray I won't have to take you up on that offer. I'm asking God for Malcolm's healing. And we know He is a healer."

CHAPTER TWENTY-FOUR

I finished talking to Lynette and went to Daddy's house to pack his belongings. With boxes in hand, I headed straight to his bedroom when I got there. I started the packing process in his closet.

While going through the closet, I found a box of old family photos. The pictures filled me with an infinite number of memories. I stopped and stared at a picture of myself when I was fourteen. I wore a red and white striped shirt and blue jeans in the picture. The outfit triggered a flashback of the day when our next-door neighbor, Mr. Billy, tried to rape me.

Mr. Billy was always friendly with us. He gave us snacks, and when Mama forced us to stay outside for hours during the summer, he always ensured we had a pitcher of ice-cold water.

One day, Mama was in one of her moods, so she forced me to stay home while the rest went to the swimming pool. She'd accused me of back-talking, which I hadn't. But she was being mean to me, as usual. I was slumping around in my misery when someone knocked on the door about five minutes after everyone left. Of course, we knew the rules—when Mama wasn't home . . don't answer the door. But once I saw it was Mr. Billy, I figured it was okay. He hesitated, looking around behind me, then asked where everyone was. I told him that they were at the swimming pool.

"They left you by yourself? No fun for you?" he said, his eyes showing excitement where the rest of his face was downturned in sympathy. "Yes," I said, my face lower than my knees.

"Well, little lady, you were going to have to share these with everyone, but now, you get to have them all to yourself."

He held up a box of doughnuts he said he'd gotten from the church. I eagerly stepped back and let him into the house. He carried the box into the kitchen. Then offering me a doughnut, Mr. Billy wanted to know how long everyone would be gone and why Mama left me home alone. "Were you being a bad girl?" he asked.

"No, sir."

"Would you like to be my bad girl?"

"No, sir," I repeated.

Mr. Billy swiftly flew at me and grabbed my shirt. Falling back, I snatched away from him so hard he ripped a hole in the right side of my shirt, but that didn't deter him. He picked me up and carried me toward the door while I kicked and screamed. I fought him hard, screaming as loud as possible. He threw me on the couch and leaped on top of me. I couldn't breathe.

He kept telling me to calm down and that he would make me feel good. At that moment, it clicked what he would do to me, so I fought even harder. Luckily, Mama forgot her coin purse and had to double back home. She ran into the house at breakneck speed when she heard me screaming.

Seeing Mr. Billy on top of me when she burst into the house, Mama swung her huge leopard skin pocketbook and hit him. Surprised, Mr. Billy let me go and jumped up, shielding himself with his hands. Mama swung harder, hitting him anywhere she could—his shoulders, back, and below the belt. Unable to protect himself from the constant blows, Mr. Billy sprinted to the front door.

A feeling of warmth and happiness flooded my heart because Mama saved me from Mr. Billy. She loved me. Still lying on the couch, I half-expected her to come and hug my visibly shaken body. But Mama gave me one of the worst beatings of my life that day. She said I knew better than to open the door for anyone, so she hit me for every word she spoke over me—a toxic word, then a blow, and so on. At the end of the day, Mama had busted my nose, left bruises on my back, and sent me to bed without dinner that night. That's when I knew that my hate for her was real.

I threw the picture back in the box. I wondered why I never told my daddy what happened. He was very protective of my sister and me. That may be why he supported Patsy the way he did.

Walking through the house, I noted how Daddy had lived in his home for a long time, but he'd recently updated it, and all its furniture was brand new. After discussing it with Malcolm and my sisters, we decided to keep the house in the family and rent it out, splitting the profits between us since Dad never remarried. He always said Mama was the love of his life before she started drinking alcohol. I remember their fights and how my dad begged her to stop drinking, but she refused. The harder he pressed, the more she drank.

Back then, I'd thought about running away so often, but I never did because I had nowhere else to go. That's when I met Malcolm, and my life changed forever.

Mama hated me, but I was always Daddy's favorite. Sometimes, I think he pitied me. He would fuss and cuss to get

Mama to ease up on me, but he couldn't control her. No one could.

Daddy told me where to find his secret stash when he left this earth: beneath the floorboards, underneath his bed, where he'd been hiding money for twenty-plus years.

I pushed the queen-sized bed out of the way and felt around. Finally finding the spot, I pulled up the board using the butter knife I'd taken from the kitchen. My mouth fell open at the sight of all the money he had stored there; it took over thirty minutes to dig out all the bags. I sat on the floor for an hour, counting until I was done. $72,231!

I planned to keep that money secret from everyone except my husband. Daddy had also left a note in one bag, dated over ten years ago. *"Spend this money wisely, Trish."*

He knew I would remember and come looking for it. It was the rainbow at the end of the storm.

I stuffed the money into the bags and carried them to the car. Then I locked up the house and left behind all the terrible childhood memories like I'd finally forgiven Mama for not loving me properly. Walking away, I knew I'd be hiring a rental manager if Bebe didn't want to do it because it was the last time, I'd ever step foot in the house again.

CHAPTER TWENTY-FIVE

On the way to MJ's courthouse wedding, Malcolm began to cough. Not comfortable with him driving, I rubbed his back and prayed as he drove. He didn't feel well, but he insisted on coming. He said he wouldn't miss this day for the world.

"Do you want to pull the car over so I can drive?" I asked him. "You don't have to be the strong man and use your energy before we get there if you don't want to alarm MJ." "No," he answered honestly. "It's nearing the time. I can feel it," he continued.

I grabbed his right hand as he held onto the steering wheel with the left.

"Are you scared?" I asked, scared myself to hear his answer.

He shook his head. "I've had a wonderful life full of love. I'll be ready to go when God is ready for me."

We reached the courthouse just as MJ and Clara started up the steps.

"Mom, Dad!" MJ beamed.

Clara was stunning. She embraced us, and we headed inside the courthouse with her parents. Their vows were beautiful. MJ left out that she was ten years older than him. Both our children fell in love with and married older mates. It was clear my son loved Clara more than she loved him. So, as the old saying goes, the man has to love you more for the relationship to work. I believed that to be true.

There was nothing but love and admiration in MJ's eyes. Clara seemed apprehensive but stood hand in hand and declared, "I do."

An hour later, at the restaurant where we held the reception, MJ clanked a spoon against a glass to get our attention.

"I know it's customary for the bride and groom to be toasted," he said, "but I want to toast my parents." He raised his glass. "The two of you are the definition of love. You taught me how to love and what love is supposed to be. Because of you, I've never been afraid to let someone in or place my heart in someone else's hands."

My eyes welled with happy tears. We did something right. He continued.

"You've made love real for me. Watching you love each other all these years has been a pleasure. I hope our marriage can be like yours, and I hope to be sitting next to Clara thirty years later, still as madly in love with her as I am today. To Mom and Dad— cheers!"

Patsy knew about Malcolm's affair, but we have yet to tell MJ. His father was his role model and MJ believed he could do no wrong.

Smiling at the bride and groom, I felt their love. I believed they would have a long, blessed marriage. But I couldn't say the same about Patsy. Thinking back on the conversation with my grandchildren, even though my daughter's relationship appeared stronger, I didn't feel she and Bounce would be together much longer.

~~~

A week after the wedding, Patsy called and asked us to keep the kids for the day so she and Bounce could have their alone time.

"I can't watch the kids today, Patsy. Your father's sick."

Malcolm had taken to bed.

"Still? It's been over a week. He may need to go to the doctor, Mama."

"Maybe," I hedged.

"I understand. Bounce and I can do a date night another time."

"I take it that things are going well between you?"

"We're working on it. So many days he looks at me like he hates me, but it is what it is." Patsy continued rambling. Then she switched up on me like someone flipped the switch to an alternate personality. "I'm feeling a little adventurous, aren't you?" she asked in a fake accent.

"Patsy? Patsy?"

"Patsy's not in at the moment, darling."

I deflated. It had been a while, but she was having an episode again.

"Patsy?"

In a singsong voice, she said, "My name is Francesca. Patsy isn't here."

Francesca was one of Patsy's personalities who'd been around the longest. Francesca was intelligent and sophisticated. I wondered if she was the personality who enjoyed sleeping with other men. Patsy's status as HIV positive could be a danger to someone out there.
~~~

"Patsy, please, hear me. Please come back," I pleaded.

"I have to go," she said and hung up the phone.

I grabbed my keys and purse. "I'm going to Patsy's house. She's having an episode," I told Malcolm. "Stay in bed, please."

Before I bolted from our bedroom, I remembered to stop and take my gun. I jumped in the car, and this time, I checked to see if bullets were inside. There were. I raced to Patsy and Bounce's house.

Things always got crazy with Patsy's other personalities. They may not have lasted long, but she was uncontrollable. Sometimes, the episodes seemed to last forever. On the other hand, Patsy had been fine for a month, so either her meds weren't working, or she missed a dose.

After breaking the speed limit to get there, I jumped from the car before it completely stopped and dashed to the back door of the house. I heard the screaming before I even opened the door. The kids were crying and Bounce had Patsy in a bear hug with her back up against his chest.

"Calm down," Bounce hollered.

"Get off me, you big buffoon! Unhand me right now!"

I hated seeing my daughter that way. No matter how often I witnessed it, it scared me. The look on Bounce's face was all too familiar. He was tired.

"Patsy?" I whispered.

"Patsy isn't here. Get out!" she screeched.

I ran around the room and found her stash of pills that she used as a backup for the shots.

"Take these."

"No!"

"Please. If you take them, I will get him to let you go."

After about five minutes of arguing and Bounce holding her against the wall, Patsy finally took the pills. Bounce tightened his grip. Patsy screamed and yelled, but he was going to hold her like that until she fell asleep. Then, when she woke up, she'd be Patsy again.

"I'll take the kids home with me," I said. Bounce nodded.

I scrambled to get the kids' things, and once I got them in the car, I returned inside and caught Patsy cursing at Bounce and trying to bite him. He just took it, holding onto her for dear life.

He loved her. "Bounce . . ."

"I got her. I'm accustomed to her episodes and know how to take care of her," he assured me.

I still didn't agree with him putting his hands on her, but watching him rock her back and forth, ignoring her insults, he earned my respect. I exhaled a long and exhausted breath. I was tired of being wrong. When I returned home, I told the kids to go to bed. They knew the routine and ran into their rooms.

When I entered our bedroom, Malcolm was passed out on the bedroom floor.

God, please, not tonight.

"Malcolm!"

"I'm okay, sweetie," he whispered. "I got a little light-headed coming back from the bathroom."

I helped him back into bed. "Do you need anything?"

"Just some rest."

I kneeled beside him in the bed and hugged him against me. "Malcolm, please, hold on a little longer. Please."

"Anything for you, Trish," he smiled.

I smiled back, and we snuggled in together. But I cried and prayed in the dark once everyone was asleep that night.

God, I need a miracle. I haven't been doing my best here lately, but I need you to touch my loved ones with your healing hands. Please give me more time with them. I need you to make us brand new. Cleanse us. Make us pure as freshly fallen snow because I need us to be who you want us to be, whole and healed. Please, help me, Lord.

CHAPTER TWENTY-SIX

The following day, I woke up to banging on the door. When I answered, two of Decatur's finest were standing there.

Oh, Lord, give me strength. This can't be good.

"Mrs. Sampson?" the taller one said. "Yes?"

"We're here to talk about your daughter, Pa—"

"What's wrong? Why are you here?" I cut off the police officer with a shaky voice. "I'm Detective Franks, and this is Officer White. Are you the parents of Patsy—"?

"Yes, I'm Trisha Sampson. My husband Malcolm Sampson, Patsy's father, is ill and in bed. What is this about?"

"Yes, Mrs. Sampson, your daughter Patsy stabbed her husband Bounce last night, ma'am. He was unresponsive when transported to the hospital. The doctors did all they could," Detective Franks said. "But it saddens me to tell you that he died this morning."

My heart dropped, and my knees buckled as I wailed, "Nooo!" This was the call I prayed I would never have for either of my children.

"May we come in?" one of them asked.

In shock, I could only nod yes as I moaned, "Why, Patsy? You were doing so well."

Once inside, Detective Franks continued to explain, "We received a call at the police station last night from a hysterical and panic-stricken female. She said her name was Patsy and she wanted to report a murder. She said someone named Francesca came into their home and stabbed her husband. His name was Bounce."

The officer paused because I cried out, knowing Patsy had done the deed. He then continued. "After arriving on the scene and being unable to locate Francesca, we found Patsy covered in blood without explaining how it got on her clothes. She said she knew the lady visited Bounce on occasion and thought they might be having an affair.

Patsy continued to insist that a lady named Francesca stabbed her husband to death. She became agitated but could not remember what had happened. Her memory faded further each time she was questioned. Finally, after breaking down uncontrollably, Patsy begged us to please call her parents."

I explained Patsy's long history of mental issues and multiple personality disorder to them.

They told me that while at the hospital, they knew her story didn't ring true and that Bounce's last words explained her condition and said it wasn't Patsy who stabbed him. It was Francesca. They then said he told Patsy he loved her before taking his last breath.

I gave the officers all the paperwork I could find on Patsy and her mental issues for the past ten years.

Malcolm appeared in the living room as I broke down and slid off the couch onto the floor. Sobbing uncontrollably, I tried to tell him what happened but was too incoherent, so Officer White explained.

Malcolm aged twenty years in less than two minutes. He

fell beside me on the floor without seeing the officers outside our home. Both gave us a look of pity as they left, advising us they'd keep us updated. And for the first time, Malcolm didn't tell me it would be okay.

CHAPTER TWENTY-SEVEN

About five months later, Patsy was allowed to call us from the mental institution. She was institutionalized by the judge and found to be incompetent to stand trial. The extensive mental health records of her dual diagnoses were a big help, along with Bounce's last words to the officers. She took it hard once what she had done had hit her, but it was the drastic pain of Bounce's death that motivated her to do the work so she could improve.

"Hey, Mama," Patsy said. I could tell she was smiling from the lilt in her voice.

"Hey, baby. How are you?" I said, matching her energy.

"I'm good and I can't wait to come home. I miss my family, especially my children. How are they holding up with both of their parents not there?"

"They're a little quieter than usual. I can't get them to talk about what happened. Your father and I try to spend more time with them and love on them. We take them to their favorite places, but they don't respond to us like they did before the incident. We're going to get all of them into therapy."

"Let me speak to them," Patsy said. I called the kids to the phone.

Sophia spoke first. In a soft voice, as if she understood the magnitude of the situation, she said, "I miss you, Mama. When are you coming home? Where's my daddy?" On the speaker, I could hear Patsy's answer. "I'll try to explain when I get home, baby. But always remember, I love you. Ask Grandma anything you need to, and she'll do her best to answer, okay?"

"Okay, I love you, Mama," Sophia replied as she passed the phone to William.

William was more animated during their conversation. "Hey, Mama! Where are you? Are you with Daddy? Can you bring me a gift when you come home? A Power Ranger or Ninja Turtle? I miss you, so if you come home, don't worry about the gifts."

Rolling her eyes at William, Paige snatched the phone from her brother's hand. Trying to be upbeat, she said in her best grown-up voice, "Hello, Mama. How are you today?"

After Patsy answered she was doing well but would need to stay there about four more weeks, Paige said, "I understand, Mama. I'm helping |Grandma take care of Sophia and William. I help with homework and try to keep them from making loud noises so Granddaddy can rest. So do what you must to come home and stay this time."

Patsy responded, "Thank you for being so mature, Paige. I'll try not to burden you with your siblings when I get home. You can then do what teenagers do."

"Don't worry, Mama, we're doing well. We want you to do the same," Paige said as she passed the phone back to me.

I smiled as each child listened to Patsy's attempt to answer their questions. But of course, they all told her they would feel better once she made it home. Although subdued, they seemed happy to talk to their mother. But they hurried off the phone.

"It's almost time to come home," Patsy shared with her

mother.

"Patsy, with your father not feeling well, I need help to watch the kids," I pointed out. "Don't worry, Mama. I'll check with my close friend Soles. I'll see if she'll help keep them. She's a certified children's therapist who practices Cognitive Behavior Therapy."

"That's good, Patsy. She sounds like she's a good and responsible person. I've been worried about the effect the situation will have on them. I know you don't want them to know about Bounce. And changing them to a school in our district has helped them not hear from their classmates about their father, and I feel like a therapist can help us break the news to them."

"I miss Bounce, Mama. I'm so sorry that Francesca did what she did. But now I have to focus on my kids. They do need therapy. Mama, after voicing my concerns in a counseling session, my therapist told me that they need the type of therapist who specializes in trauma experienced by children. Let me read to you from the pamphlet they gave me. It reads that a children's therapist will help them improve children's moods, anxiety, and behavior. Mama, they'll help them by examining their confusion about what happened between Bounce and me. First, they will teach them that thoughts cause feelings and attitudes, which can influence behavior. Then she will help them identify and replace harmful thought patterns with more appropriate feelings and behaviors."

"That's good, Patsy."

"Mama, the therapist, said she would listen to them and offer helpful suggestions for their well-being when I got home."

"I don't think we should wait until you get home, Patsy. I

know you're doing well, but the courts must finalize your release. I can find someone exactly like you just stated so the children can get the help they need now, or your friend Soles can help find someone. I don't want them to grow up broken from what they witnessed in their young lives."

"Okay, Mama. I'll send you this pamphlet."

"I also wanted you to know that your dad and I will be out of town for the next two weeks. We will be in Costa Rica. Do you think your friend can help with the kids, or will I need to use your aunt Bebe?"

"She'll help, Mama. She's the only one who has written me since I've been here, and the kids love her and her kids."

"That's great. Have her call me."

"Sure will, Mama. You and Dad deserve this break. Thank you for all you've done."

"As long as you're okay, that's thanks enough for me. That's why God created the family."

"I'm going to be better. I'm going to be a normal and exceptional mother. You never gave up on me and I am so grateful."

"I'll always be here for you, Patsy. And I'll always have your back." And I meant every word.

For years, Patsy asked for more potent medication. It was a shame that it took this horrible incident for her to get the help she needed. But at least she had it now.

"Well, we need to get ready to go. I have to drop the children off at church."

"Goodbye, Mama. See you soon."

I didn't have the heart to tell her that Malcolm was on his last leg when a clinical trial suddenly became available, and he was the perfect candidate. He still has cancer; however, the trial drugs slowed it down. Then, finally, he had more time and felt better than ever. Even though doctors were unsure when or if the drugs would stop working, it was a relief that the cancer wasn't spreading, and for the time being, the symptoms had all but diminished.

However, the doctors warned Malcolm that the drugs could simply stop working one day, and he could die. So, in the meantime, we promised to use the time we had to live every day like it was his last.

A little while later, my phone rang, and it was Patsy's friend, Soles. She said she'd be glad to take the kids and that her kids had missed them. She promised that her kids didn't know about Bounce and that her extended family loved Patsy and the kids and would welcome them with open arms.

In the end, Soles stepped up in a major way to help us with the kids. Unknown to us, Patsy had developed her own village to assist with her family, and she had us. Sometimes, all it takes is one good friend.

CHAPTER TWENTY-EIGHT

I joined a new church and I loved it. One Sunday, I sat in the pew when the pastor said, "If we don't forgive, we have no avenue to get to heaven." That's when the Holy Spirit spoke to me and revealed a three- step process for finding freedom through forgiveness. I called it my "BAA"—the cry of a lost lamb looking at her heavenly Father for help finding her way back to Him and healing the wounds she's received. I began teaching Bible study on forgiveness using the BAA process at the new church.

B. Breathe

This process begins with a B: breathe.

> 1. Breathe in God's love.
> 2. Breathe out the pain and the hurt.
> 3. Breathe in God's Holy Spirit and His forgiveness.
> 4. Breathe out the anger and the grief.

Breathe in gratitude for this moment where you have recognized your need to forgive and your need for forgiveness. Breathe out any resentment you carried for the things that happened to you.

Breathe in trust that God will work all things for your good and His glory. Breathe out any worry or anxiety for the future you have been allowing to color your decisions.

Breathe in God's promise that He has plans to prosper and not harm you, to give you hope and a future. Breathe out the lies you've believed; nothing good could come from what happened to you. It already is.

Breathe in God's promise that He will always be there for you and never abandon or leave you orphaned. Breathe out the fear of abandonment and rejection.

Keep breathing in God's life, love, and Holy Spirit as you transition to the next phase.

A. Ask

Ask for the Holy Spirit's guidance in showing you what you need to forgive others for doing and what you need to ask His forgiveness for what you have done.

During this second stage, grab a box of tissues and prepare yourself for what the Holy Spirit reveals. This is where the Holy Spirit leads you back into the past to help you understand why you were doing what you were doing.

A heart filled with unforgiveness, anger, and bitterness is like the tomb where Christ lay. It's as if He is dead in us and we need the reverse to happen. We need to die to ourselves and allow Him to takeover. He can only work on us if we remain that way. To open us up to forgiveness, the Holy Spirit must roll away the stone that has formed over our hearts and break it wide open.

That process brings pain and tears will roll, but those tears and that pain is like the surgeon's scalpel that brings healing after the pain is over. Upon completion of this phase, you are ready for phase three.

A. Accept

This is often the most challenging phase of the forgiveness journey, but when you reach this stage, it is time to accept forgiveness. If you're like me, that will be challenging. I certainly didn't feel like I deserved it.

Based on the forgiveness model, I knew I had to release all the bitterness and unforgiveness. So, I let it all go. The anger and unforgiveness. I let go and let God take control. I forgave Dianna, Carolyn, and the most important person of all, I forgave myself.

~~~

It was a beautiful April day and the flowers bloomed all around. Trees sang and danced in the light breeze. For months, it seemed like I was losing everything, my family, my friends, and myself. But the Holy Spirit told me, "Trish, search your heart for the bitter root spirit that caused you to damage your family. Stop and ask God to forgive you for your role in the saga."

Choosing to forgive is the most potent antidote for the pain caused by myself or others. However, forgiveness does not mean simply forgiving and forgetting. Nor does forgiveness mean absolving the person of their actions. Instead, forgiveness is letting go of anger and choosing compassion, releasing the desire to punish someone or yourself for an offense.

Bible study that first night was a success. I taught about forgiveness and love while sharing my journey with others, then headed home to my husband. When I pulled into the driveway, waiting for me was a familiar face. Carolyn was sitting on my front porch.
~~~

I eased from the car and slowly ambled to the porch while searching Carolyn's eyes to determine her emotional state.

"Hi, Trish," Carolyn said with trepidation.

Before she could finish her sentence, I embraced her.

"I forgive you. I forgive you, my friend," I sobbed.

Carolyn hugged me as she wept. "I missed you so much."

"I missed you too," I said. "I forgive you and want you to be part of my life. You are my best friend, and I need you."

With tears streaming down her face, Carolyn said, "I missed you too. I'm so sorry. I'll never do anything to mess up our friendship again."

"I know. And I won't be so unforgiving."

I wiped the tears from her face and discussed the forgiveness model. Not only that, but I vowed we must practice forgiveness as a lifestyle.

"So, you moved to Tennessee? And now you're back?"

"Girl, I missed home. It's too slow there for me. I've been back for a couple of days. I wasn't sure if I would come by, especially after hearing what happened with Patsy and Bounce."

"Patsy's doing so much better and she's about to come home, Lord willing. The medical report will have to go before the courts, but everyone feels it will only be a matter of going through the process. And for Bounce's sacrifice, she is determined to stay on her meds and improve. I hate what happened, but she finally got the help and medicine she needed. I think she's going to be okay from now on."

"That's so good to hear." Carolyn smiled and brushed her hand against her cheek.

I saw a sparkle and grinned wide. "Oh my goodness! You're getting married?"

"Yes, girl. And he came back with me. He's so good to me. I love him," she gushed.

"I'm thrilled for you."

"Thank you, and I want you to be my matron of honor."

"Of course. Tell me all about him!"

Carolyn and I ended up talking for hours. We had so much to catch up on. I was so glad she came home and happy to have her back in my life. A good friend is hard to find. I couldn't believe I almost let her go and nearly let unforgiveness make me miss our genuine friendship.

God works mysteriously and always answers prayers. This reunion with Carolyn was what I prayed for.

"My heart is full," I said, lying in Malcolm's arms later that night.

"I know."

"I missed Carolyn." "I know."

"And I'm so happy Patsy is doing better. I can't wait for her to come home."

"Do you think she'll ever get over what she did?"

"I think she already understood it wasn't her and that Bounce knew that too." I exhaled.

"I'm glad things aren't as bad as they could've been. They could've charged her with murder or locked her away for the rest of her life. I thank God for Bounce's last words. The doctors and nurses testifying to what he said helped her."

Bounce spent his last breath to ensure he protected Patsy because he loved her that much. And once I understood the truth, despite all that happened between them, I thanked God for allowing Bounce to love Patsy with all his heart.

"She's going to be better than ever. I can feel it."

"Me too," Malcolm said, rubbing his leg.

"How are you feeling?" "I feel fine."

"Fine, or—" Malcolm kissed me, then we made love.

The following day, we boarded our flight to Costa Rica. My husband and I enjoyed every activity under the sun for two weeks. We created memories and shared special moments. Our love grew more potent than ever before. I saw Malcolm smiling and enjoying himself, which was all I could ask.

"Let's watch the sunrise. It is our last day in paradise," he said.

As we watched the beautiful sunrise, Malcolm's phone pinged. After reading the message, he passed his phone to me with trembling hands and tear-filled eyes. Then in an enthusiastic voice, he asked me to read an email from his doctor. I braced myself for the unwelcome news.

"It's a miracle!" I exclaimed. "Your scans came back, and the treatment is working! Oh my God! God is so good! The tumor is shrinking! It's working!"

Malcolm grabbed the phone and wept. He hadn't shed a tear throughout this entire process until that moment. I could only assume he was relieved that he may have more time left on this earth than he'd thought. "God, I thank you!" I praised God right there. He was healing my husband and I couldn't be more thankful. God is an awesome God, kind and just. "Thank you for showing my husband and me a little favor," I told Him.

We made our way to the beach to watch the sunrise.

My cell phone rang, and I noticed it was the mental institution.

"Mama, I'm leaving. I'm going home," Patsy said.

God, look at you showing out! "Are you ready, Patsy?"

"Yes, Mama. I'm ready. I can do this.

I will be better this time." "Okay. Let's do this!"

Patsy and the kids were moving in with us. I wanted to ensure her stability before sending her home with three kids alone. "Our flight leaves soon. We will be home sometime overnight."

"Okay, I will be there waiting." "I love you, Patsy."

"I love you too." My husband healed! My daughter healed! My heart was full!

See, God will give abundantly in return when we give a little. He will bless you. You just need to trust him. I resolved never to stray and to always believe in and trusted God's plan.

"Patsy is going home," I told Malcolm the news when I hung up.

He smiled. "I love you, Trish." I took a deep breath.

Forgiveness is a test. Forgiveness is game. I won.

"Always and forever," I said to my husband.

Forever was looking surprisingly good to me.

THE END

Support & Resources

Domestic violence, addictions/alcoholism, and Mental Health are serious areas of concern in many families. Within African American communities we have traditionally discounted these oftentimes generational concerns. If you or someone you know is suffering from or needs assistance due to domestic violence, addiction, or mental health disorders, please contact any of the agencies listed here to assist.

Alcoholics Anonymous 24-Hour Hotline:
1-856-486-4444
www.aa.org

American Psychiatric Association:
1-800-847-3802
psychiatry.org/patients-families

National Domestic Violence 24-Hour Hotline:
1-800-799-7233
www.thehotline.org

Sex Addicts Anonymous 24/7 Hotline:
1-800-477-8191
www.saa-recovery.org

Substance Abuse and Mental Health
Services Administration (24/7):
1-800-662-4357
www.samhsa.org

Childhelp National Child Abuse Hotline
1-800-422-4453
childhelphotline.org

Crisis Support Ministry New Life
Bible Church, Fayetteville, NC
910-868-9640

About The Author

Dr. Norma McLauchlin is the proud Curator of TEDx Hoke Loop Road and a member of the Forbes Business Council. She is the owner and CEO of Chosen Pen Publishing, Forgiveness Across Borders, and Chosen 2 Thrive in the United States and aboard. As a TEDx and Forbes speaker, McLauchlin is an international bestselling author, publisher, and speaker. In her role as certified master literary consultant and writing coach, she is fondly known as "First Lady" in and around her community as well as abroad where she has helped establish literacy programs and forgiveness gardens in two South African primary schools. She inspires individuals to embrace spiritual change and live more fulfilling lives. Dr. McLauchlin earned a BSBA from Fayetteville State University, a Master's from Central Michigan University, an MBA from Virginia Technical and State University, and a Doctor of Education from North Carolina State University.

Follow Dr. McLauchlin and Chosen Pen Publishing by visiting:

Instagram @chosenpenpublishing

Twitter @NormaMcLauchlin

Facebook @chosenpublishing

Email firstladynorma@chosepen.com

Web www.chosepen.com
https://linktr.ee/@NormaMcLauchlin

www.ingramcontent.com/pod-product-compliance
Lightning Source LLC
Chambersburg PA
CBHW061305210726
48293CB00003B/1119